Unreal Time

MARTII MACLEAN

Published by Kooky Cat Books 2018

Copyright © 2018 Martii Maclean

www.martiimaclean.com

Book cover design and formatting services by BookCoverCafe.com

First edition 2018

ISBN
978-0-9945408-8-1 (pbk)
978-0-9945408-9-8 (e-bk)

For Trevor and Minerva, my extraordinary companions.
Travelling with me through time.
Always by my side as we face fearsome and fantastic
happenings together.

Prologue

Link whistled up into the trees, and the dense rainforest canopy shook above him. He whistled again, and from somewhere hidden in the green, Rex chittered. His furry snout and shiny eyes appeared out of the leaves and he dropped into full view, dangling, tail coiled around the branch.

'Get here, come on,' Link called, patting his thigh.

Rex stared down at Link, chittered, then swung, flipped in the air and landed, claws digging into the tree's thick bark. Scuttling around, he pointed his shiny nose to the ground and bounded down the trunk, front paws clinging and rear end hopping. Link always expected the quollago to bounce right off the tree as he descended, but he never did.

'Got to love genetic modification,' he said, as Rex leapt the last two metres to the ground and rolled over, wagging his fluffy, coiled tail and pawing the air, waiting for a scratch.

'How's my little hybrid goin'?' Link squatted and scratched Rex's belly. Then he froze. Rex chittered his complaints and wriggled under Link's frozen hand. Link continued to stare out at nothing as his mind was redirected, linking to Node.

<<message> :: temporal scoop operational and powered :: DNA tag loaded :: request retrieval Neil Nifty Banks ASAP :: organise your team :: data package sending now :: < end>>

Link's eyes brightened again and Rex squirmed as the scratching recommenced. 'Tonight's the night, Rex. Node's sending us to retrieve Nifty.'

Rex sensed Link's excitement and jumped up, licking his face, huffing hot breath all over him.

Link wriggled his nose at the smell: a mango, eucalyptus and mystery-meat combo. 'Let's go, boy. We better tell the others.'

Same Start, Different Day

The phone glowed to life on the table next to Deon's bed. He'd forgotten to turn it off last night. *Bleep. Bleep. Bleep. Bleep. Bleep.* His stomach lurched with each new message he received. It was only seven am and they'd started already. He knew he should delete the messages without looking, but usually he couldn't. It would be the same old crud: nerd jokes, insults, and threats to make him a dodge-ball target.

He wanted to commit another phone flush. It had given him some peace last time, until his mum had brought him a replacement. Then it all started again. But his mum would suspect a second phone flush as a too-odd coincidence, and then she might clue in and Deon didn't want her worrying about the kids at his new school. She had enough going on.

'Quark.' He reached over and turned the off the notification sounds before flicking through a few of the photos on the phone. He missed his mates from his old life in the city. *Humans.*

3

He smiled, looking at a photo of himself smiling back, surrounded by the friendly faces of his mates. They were huddled around a robot they'd built for a technology festival. The robot was holding up the trophy they'd won that day. There had been so many projects and experiments and trophies just like that one. Deon had left all of that behind when he and his mum had packed up and left the city.

The kids here at Moran's Cove were like another species to Deon. When he'd first arrived at Moran's Cove High, he'd done what he always did: dived straight into his work and answered the teachers' questions. Then he noticed one day in his maths class that everyone was staring at him and the teacher was smiling, as though he'd found buried treasure. Deon realised that he was the only student in the room who was saying anything—apart from some mumbled jokes and one-liners. So he backtracked, playing dumb to stop himself becoming too noticeable before he could figure this place out.

Moving to Moran's Cove had been something Deon had both wanted and not wanted. His old house in the city would always be the place where his dad had died. It was filled with sad memories. In the time after the doctors said *cancer*, it was like his dad had begun a weird, backwards evolution of man. His dad had always been smarter and funnier than anyone. He'd always stood strong and tall, but as he got sicker, he became stooped and began to curl in on himself, diminishing. He ended up becoming nothing like the man he had once been.

Over those weeks, as his dad got sicker, Deon had watched his mum holding his dad's hand and holding her breath, smiling, making things as okay as she could for them all.

Even though Deon knew his dad was going to die, when it happened it was like a punch in the chest. He imagined that he would always feel a giant kind of lonely. He wanted to find a way to live forever so nothing like that would ever happen to him.

After the funeral was over and all the well-wishers had faded away, his mum seemed to start fading away, too. Being in that house without his dad seemed to dissolve her. She looked thin and transparent. Not long after that, his mum announced that they were moving to Moran's Cove.

Dad's brother, Deon's uncle Nifty, had moved to the Cove after he had retired from the military. Nifty wasn't old or anything, and he wouldn't give any reasons why. He just announced one day that he was retiring and moving to Moran's Cove. He and Deon's dad had spent holidays there when they were young, but Deon knew that even his dad had wondered what the big attraction was for Nifty.

Nifty had been determined. 'It just feels like the right move,' was all he said.

Then it was Deon's mum's turn. She was equally determined that this was the right move for them. 'It's important to be with family,' she said. 'Your uncle Nifty lives there. Your dad and you used to do that genius-brain thing together, and I know you need that. You miss it.'

5

She was right. Deon badly missed his dad's 'think-fests', as he'd called them, but Deon would also really miss his life in the city.

What about my friends here? I've known them forever. Deon only said this inside his head. He knew they both needed to get away from all the sadness in that house, and strangely, he also felt drawn to Moran's Cove for some reason. Maybe he just missed Nifty.

They'd moved, and the giant lonely from losing his dad had started shrinking, but now it was surrounded by the smaller solitudes caused by being in a new school and a new town. So life went from sad to impossible. Moran's Cove High was not a good place to be if you didn't surf, and worse, it was a very bad place to be if you knew stuff and answered questions in class.

Deon couldn't remember a time when he didn't know stuff. Since he was very small it had always seemed like he knew lots of things about everything, and if he didn't know it, then he knew how and where to find the information he wanted.

Once Deon was old enough for the think-fest, his dad would pose questions. The hours would fly by as they explored ideas and searched through books and online, trying to win arguments and claim discoveries.

Once, when Nifty was visiting, Mum had walked into the kitchen wearing sunglasses and zinc on her nose.

'Why?' Deon had asked, smiling.

'Well, with you three all thinking together I'm beginning to see a glow. I wouldn't want to get a nasty burn from all that brilliance radiating out from your heads.'

That was the one cool thing about moving to Moran's Cove. Nifty seemed to know when Deon needed a deep think, and he would pose a juicy question or a challenge, and the think-fest would be on. Nifty had worked for the government as some kind of 'brain for hire', as he called it. Now he was retired, but he still kept a shed full of projects. Some of them he still kept secret, but some things in the shed became part of the think-fests.

Getting used to how different things were in Moran's Cove and at school had been problematic at first, but Deon soon managed to develop a sort of invisibility. The kids had left him alone for a while, but that had changed a few weeks ago. All eyes were on him again. He had lost his social cloaking device.

At Deon's old school, answering the teacher's questions was a very small deal, but at Moran's Cove it was different. He discovered that during the first maths lesson, before he knew better. Knowing stuff and answering questions resulted in a very different reaction at this high school.

All he'd done was answer Mr Novak's problem-of-the-day question, but there had been a ripple of snorts and whispers around the room. Deon had managed to convince them it was a fluke, and then he kept a low profile for a few weeks.

He spent time watching everyone and learning. He felt like an anthropologist discovering a new species. 'Homo sapiens zombie,' he'd jokingly mumble to himself. Could there even be such a classification?

Deon didn't think that all people who chose to surf were dumb—the other surfers he'd met around town seemed clever, thoughtful, normal H. sapiens—but Deon's surf-zombie classmates were definitely the exception. They were impressive when they took to the waves, but their only skill on dry land was waxing their boards.

'Not an accurate observation,' he told himself, using his David Attenborough voice. They all appeared to have part-time jobs to earn money to buy more surf gear.

He'd been sure that if he just stayed away from these single-minded surf zombies he could blend into the background, but that had only worked until the records from his old school arrived and found their way into Mr Novak's hands.

Deon decided that his poor maths teacher must have been starved for a student that knew more than how to read a tide chart. Mr Novak went out of his way to let Deon know how pleased he was to read the records and the proof they contained about the smartness Deon had been working so hard to hide since arriving at the school.

One morning, at the end of another maths lesson, Deon had been trying to slide invisibly out of the room when Mr Novak looked up from what he was reading. He stood and moved to block Deon's path. He was holding a folder with Deon's name on it.

'Banks … Deon, I just looked at the records from your old school,' Mr Novak said, flapping the folder with excitement. 'You've won a fairly impressive collection of awards and competitions. Not to mention the Robot Team Challenge.'

At that moment, Johno Staples and his buddies walked past the open door. Time seemed to slow down. Johno stopped and tilted his head to listen.

'Um, thanks, sir,' Deon said, almost choking on his reply.

'Well, no wonder you could do my daily challenge on that first day, Banks. But don't be shy. You haven't had much to say in class for weeks. Now that I've seen all these awards in your file, I'll up the ante a bit.' Deon cringed as Mr Novak patted him roughly on the shoulder and took another hungry look inside the folder.

The guys were standing in the doorway watching and listening as Mr Novak blabbed on, drooling over Deon's file like a newly discovered treasure, mumbling about posing special maths problems. Suddenly Deon was no longer invisible.

Johno and his shamble of surf zombies had heard it all, and as soon as Mr Novak left the classroom it started.

'Hey, brainiac,' Johno said, 'did I hear Novak say you're a genius?'

'We're really sorry we put the hard word on you to surf when you first got here,' droned another of the zombies.

'Yeah, sorry,' another voice echoed.

'We know you wouldn't have learned to surf in the city. You wouldn't have time, with all that thinkin' and kissin' judges' butts at competitions. You probably never even learned to swim.'

'Hey, Johno,' grunted Pete, another member of the gang, 'maybe with all those extra brains in his head, it's too heavy, and when he tries to swim his giant brain sinks and his butt floats up to the surface.'

9

The zombies exploded with snorts and laughter.

'At least that would give me a reason for surfing badly,' said Deon. 'What's yours?'

'Oooh, ladies and gentlemen,' Pete said, 'we have a winner.'

Deon cringed. He mumbled the multipurpose curse word his old robot team always used: 'Quark.' Today was not going to be a good day.

'Your prize, brainiac, is us,' said Johno. 'You get us for the rest of this day, which could end up being the worst day of your life.'

'Winner, winner, winner,' the zombies chanted.

They squeezed in around him, nudging him along the corridor and shoving him into the locker room, where they pinned him up against his locker, then gave the metal door a thorough kicking.

'Maybe your big brainy head will be the next thing we kick, nerd boy,' said Johno.

The bell went and they scattered, leaving Deon to wonder how much the school would charge for the repairs to his dented locker door.

Since that day, Deon had had to try even harder to either blend in or hide out. His blood boiled with the unfairness of it all. Stuck here, all alone, at Moran's Cove. He still had his mates from the city. He could call them when he didn't flush his phone, and his mum would still arrange for him to do some competitions, which was cool. But over the past few weeks, ever since Mr Novak had revealed his secret, Deon had spent masses of time trying to figure out how to survive in his new hometown.

The phone taunted Deon, glowing with each new message that arrived while he got dressed. His stomach fought against his breakfast as he forced himself to eat while his mum hummed and cleaned her brushes and other art stuff in the kitchen sink. She hadn't seemed happy for a long time. Deon liked that she was humming again, so he wasn't going to tell her what was going on at school. He tried pushing all that from his mind, and walked, lead-footed, to the bus stop. Every now and then his phone vibrated in his pocket and reminded him.

The day went better than Deon thought it would until last period, maths.

'Banks, am I right?' said the tower of brown corduroy that was Mr Novak. The board was filled with a massive problem.

'Not sure, sir,' mumbled Deon. *Thanks for reminding Johno and his zombies that I exist minutes before I've got to get on the bus with them.*

Mr Novak smirked. 'Told you I'd up the ante, Banks.'

'You have no idea how much, sir,' mumbled Deon, glancing at Johno.

'I have an idea,' Johno whispered behind Deon as the home bell sounded. 'See you on the bus, brainiac."

Scooped

The bus rocked from side to side as it struggled along the old highway back to town. The road was not particularly rough or potholed. The rocking was caused by the zombies playing a new game they called 'brainiac ball'. The object of the game was to use schoolbags as the ball and Deon's head as a goalpost.

'Hey, you morons, cut that out or I'll stop the bus.'

Deon looked towards the voice for a second. He could see the driver's frustrated red face reflected in the mirror. The driver looked the way Deon felt—like he really wanted the bus trip to be over.

Deon copped one last goal in the face as the bus reached his stop. He grabbed his bag and dove for the back door, flying out onto the footpath like something under pressure. He had survived another day, just. He shrugged his bag onto his shoulders and jogged away from the bus stop.

As he ran home, he quickly calculated how many more school days lay between this moment and the end of year twelve. Five hundred and seventeen more days that would probably be a lot like this one, unless he got lucky and was kidnapped by aliens.

'Hi, best mum in the world,' he said with forced happiness, as he ran in the back door and through the kitchen.

'How was your—'

He waved as he flashed past and quickly disappeared into his room so he didn't have to share the shabby details about school and the zombies. His mum didn't need the hassle, not now she was smiling. He would talk it out with his uncle Nifty, soon.

Minutes later, he waved again as he went past her in the other direction, dressed for a run. 'Love your work, Mum,' he said. 'Back for dinner.'

'Love you, too,' her voice called over the slam of the screen door.

He hadn't wanted to stay long enough in the kitchen to get a drink, and his tongue felt like sandpaper. He grabbed the hose as he crossed the backyard, turned it on and waited until the water ran cool. He stuck the end into his mouth, slurping a huge drink.

His mum was pretty cool. She didn't make him do all that 'what are you thinking' stuff that some mothers did. She had been letting him figure it all out for himself since his dad died. Deon *was* working things out about his dad, but he was fine with letting her think it was all about Dad. He would figure out the school thing. It wouldn't last forever.

The only thing constant is change, Deon thought, echoing Heraclitus.

His dad had liked to quote the Greek philosophers. Deon smiled at the memory. Things would change soon enough.

He looped the hose around the tap and jogged down the driveway, concentrating on setting the pace for his run. Johno and the surf zombies would already be heading for the beach, so if he headed to the other side of town he should have an uneventful run and be able to clear his head. He often ran along the old showground road and out to the broken telegraph pole at the top of the hill.

His feet pounded on the road, the rhythm jolting up through his body. Back in the city, his dad used to run with him, before he got sick. Deon imagined he could hear his dad breathing hard beside him. *I miss you, Dad.* He sighed and pushed harder, heading out of town. Maybe he would drop in at Nifty's place after the run and tell him what was happening at school. Maybe.

Deon often showed up at Nifty's giant shed and just sat there, sort of soaking in the stuff about his uncle that reminded him of his dad. Nifty let him hang around. They both knew how hard it was. Like Deon's mum, Nifty didn't ask how Deon was feeling; they just hung out together. Deon could let the feelings about his dad not be a big deal, even though they were.

At Nifty's shed, there were only two rules: if Deon used something he had to put it back where he found it, and he was never to go into the storeroom, not that Deon could have managed that because it was always locked tight. Nifty was retired, sort of. In the military, his job had been to build things he could never talk about.

Sometimes when Deon was watching the news with Nifty and a story about a new invention came on, Nifty would quietly say, 'I helped develop that one.' Then he'd shrug and say, 'I couldn't tell you about it. We had to keep it a secret until they decided it didn't have to be a secret anymore.'

Deon's feet pounded out a comforting rhythm as he turned onto the road that ran past the showgrounds. Heading away from the water was always the best way to ensure he wouldn't run into any of the kids from school. Everyone always hung out at the beach, or at the shops, so it was usually just him, the road, and the rhythm of his heartbeat.

He felt the strain of the day fading away with every puffing breath. The afternoon breeze was cool on his sweaty face. The road veered to the southwest. The trees on the roadside made a patchwork of shade and light as the sun dipped low in the sky, with the refraction through the atmosphere making it appear to be growing fat before fading to orange.

The muscles in his legs warmed and his breathing grew faster as the road started to slope upwards, away from the low-lying ground of the shore and mangroves, and into the hills that buttressed the jagged cliffs to the west of town. He looked up towards the waterfall in the far distance. It looked like a set of giant steps. He felt small when he compared himself to the landscape towering around him, but he kept his focus on the top of the next hill.

He could just see what remained of the broken telegraph pole that was his regular turnaround point, looking like a stick in the distance and blurred by the haze shimmering off the road.

Deon thought it was a bit late in the day for there still to be a heat haze, but the trees had been cleared away for the power lines, and with less shade on the road, maybe the bitumen was still hot enough up there for the miasma to remain.

Deon thumped on: *thump*; feet, *thump*; heart. His head became clearer with every breath.

The broken pole grew thicker and taller, and the heat haze still danced on the hill. Dark shapes were slithering around inside the glinting haze, as though people were waving or dancing behind the pole.

He liked the idea of mirages, and watched this one as he ran. He knew that travellers in the desert could be convinced to wander off track to their doom, believing they saw what they so badly wanted to see in a mirage. Deon knew the haze would disappear when he moved closer to it. Every high-school science student understood how mirages worked. Well, maybe not here in Moran's Cove, he thought.

He dropped his head and focused on his feet. His heart walloped against his ribs as he put on power for the climb to the top of the hill. The burning in his legs, and the stubble of dried grass at the roadside, let him know he was nearly at the pole.

He looked up; the haze remained. Weird. Science didn't usually break its own rules.

The dark figures were also still present in the haze.

'My own personal mirage,' he muttered.

The pole now seemed to be *behind* the haze.

As Deon reached out his hand to touch the pole, he moved through the haze that shouldn't be there and a wave of dizziness hit him. His vision darkened and was filled with splotches of colour. He felt everything tilting, as if he was still on the bus, being jolted sideways and slammed by a flying bag in a moronic game of brainiac-ball.

He fell, sprawling on the hard ground. The air was knocked out of him as he landed. Groaning as he rolled onto his back, he tried to catch his breath. The air was cold, prickling his sweaty skin. With his eyes half open, he could see that the sun had set and the sky was dark.

'Must've knocked myself out when I tripped.'

'Not tripped,' said a singsong voice somewhere behind Deon, 'scooped—over.'

Deon's body tensed, ready for trouble, just like at school.

'Shush, Bump. You shouldn't speak to Nifty like that,' said a serious female voice to Deon's left.

'Sorry, just excited—over and out.'

Deon struggled to see what was happening through the swirling splotches that still sparked across his vision. Each time he moved, his head crackled with static, like when he touched a car door and got a shock.

'Out of the way, you two,' came a third voice, male, young. 'Welcome. Please excuse all the excitement. We've been trying for a very long time to get you here. It's a great and exciting thing to finally scoop Nifty. I hope the scoop wasn't too uncomfortable for you.'

Deon opened his eyes wide. Leaning over him was a smiling, tanned face, framed by coils of sandy coloured hair. A strange, bulky necklace made up of shiny square plaques that looked like a string of small black touchscreens hung around the figure's neck.

The smiling face reached out a hand. 'I'm Link. Welcome, Nifty.'

'Welcome, Nifty,' chorused four or five other shadowy faces that appeared out of the darkness and loomed over Deon. They all wore the same strange jewellery around their necks.

'I'm not Nifty,' said Deon, coughing. His throat was still dry from running.

'Not Nifty!' the voices said in unison.

'Not Nifty—over,' echoed a single voice.

'But Node gave the DNA code,' said Link. 'The scoop doesn't work unless you've got the right code. One moment, checking data.' His eyes became glassy and he mumbled to himself for a while.

'Nifty is my uncle, Neil Banks. Is this some weird military thing? He's retired, you know.' Deon struggled to sit up. His head still sparked and spun with that strange static dizziness.

Link stood in front of him, staring and making incoherent sounds. The rest of the group was circling them. A mumbled chant was growing steadily louder.

'Not Nifty, not Nifty, not Nifty, not Nifty, not Nifty, not Nifty ...'

The chanting and the circling made Deon's dizziness and nausea worse. He tried to grab hold of some tuffs of grass to steady himself. He was getting ready to throw up.

Link's eyes suddenly refocused. He looked past Deon and spoke to the others. 'Node says to reject with urgency and retry with caution. Power up the scoop.'

'Powering,' said the female voice from somewhere in the darkness.

Deon heard a buzzing sound, and felt the static building up around him again.

Link crouched in front of him and held out his hand. 'Nothing personal, mate, you're just not the one we need.'

Deon took the outstretched hand. 'Ouch!'

Link dug one of his fingernails into Deon's palm, scratching him deeply. 'Again, nothing personal, Node said to check the codes,' he said with a smile. Then he stood up, wrapped the finger that had scratched Deon in a piece of shiny cloth, put both hands into his pockets and walked into the gloom outside the circle of dull light.

A shadowy figure bent over and stuck his face into Deon's. 'Not Nifty,' he snapped, 'over and *out*!'

Deon felt the static around him pull-push on his body. His brain crackled, everything around him flipped and spun, and then the pull-push released its grip on him. He lay in the dirt, looking up at the broken telegraph pole silhouetted against the blinding orange of the setting sun. A moment ago it had been dark. What just happened?

He rolled over, lifted himself onto one elbow, and vomited onto the dust at the base of the splintered telegraph pole.

Fess Up

Deon took it very slowly as he headed for his uncle Nifty's house. With each plodding step, his head sparked and the weird chant echoed in his mind: *Not Nifty, not Nifty …* By the time he got to Nifty's shed, what had happened at the pole was still swirling around in his mind—the dark, the static. *Sorry, mate, nothing personal.* Deon flexed his scratched palm and winced. The wound was real, but how could the rest of it be?

Nifty's shed was as big as some people's whole backyards, and had security cameras. The first time Deon had looked up and seen the cameras, he'd been full of curiosity and a little suspicion.

'You're not really retired, are you, Nifty?' he had asked, pointing at the glinting mechanical eyes.

'Well, Deon, sometimes you become part of something in a way that means you can never really walk away from it,' Nifty had said. He had a way of giving answers that left things unanswered. Deon imagined that Nifty had been trained in giving non-answers as part of his old job.

Taking a huge calming breath, Deon stepped into the warm light inside his uncle's mega shed. As usual, the air was filled with one of the songs from Nifty's nineties playlist. 'Hey, Nifty,' he called into the forest of techie equipment, 'is that the Peppers?' Deon pointed to the speaker on the wall.

'Deon! You make your uncle proud, recognising songs from my stellar playlist.' Nifty swooped over, grabbed Deon and started doing his goofy hug dance, singing, 'Huggy-hug-hug-huuug.'

Nifty could be random like that. He used to do it all the time when Deon was little. It was hilarious when Nifty had done the huggy dance with Deon's dad. Deon would sit back, looking on and laughing his head off as he watched his dad being jiggled around by his brother, his arms trapped by his sides. 'Huggy-hug-hug-huuug.'

Deon's face was pushed against Nifty's warm jumper. 'Hey, Nifty, I'm not little anymore.' Deon felt like he was in a malfunctioning tumble dryer. He sighed and surrendered to the huggy dance.

'Hugg-hug-hug-huuug,' Nifty sang, until they both fell on the floor laughing.

'You might be too old for the huggy dance, but I never will be, so thank you for dancing with your uncle anyway. I appreciate it.' Nifty stood up and bowed. Deon thought he looked like some foppish courtier at a medieval ball. Nifty took Deon's hand and puckered up like he would kiss it.

'Random,' said Deon.

'Random is my middle name,' Nifty said.

He stopped puckering and moved to a bench where Deon had left a dismantled running timer he had been repairing. 'Come look at this,' Nifty said. 'You did a good job on it. I'm just putting it back together again.'

Nifty had been teaching Deon how to make and repair all kinds of things since he and his mum had moved to Moran's Cove, and Deon appreciated the projects on offer. He needed to have something more challenging than schoolwork to think about. He especially appreciated having something to block out thoughts of his dad, and missing his old school, and his old life. Running helped, but he couldn't run all the time.

'All finished,' said Nifty, after a few minutes. 'You did a great job, Deon. You have a real knack for innovation. At this rate, in a few years that knack will turn into pure invention.'

'Thanks, Nifty.' Deon shrugged. 'I like having my mind occupied.'

Nifty turned to face Deon, his voice becoming gentle. 'Hey, sorry, boy genius, I do get a bit mad professor sometimes, don't I? I know it's hard. I can't stop thinking about Mick—your dad—either. You okay?'

'Yeah, I'm good, and thanks, Nifty. I really like the fixing, the inventing. I'm not being a poser, but it's good to have somewhere to be able to be smart without having to hide it. Moron's Cove High is—'

'Moron's Cove.' Nifty laughed. 'School's a bit tough, then, hey?'

'Well, yeah, but the zombies—'

'Zombies?'

'Johno and his henchmen.'

Nifty shrugged.

'A few guys at school,' Deon said. 'They're like zombies—you know, low brain function, obsessed with pursuing their target. Unfortunately, I've become their target lately. It's cool. They'll get bored, it won't last long.' Deon shook his head. 'But it's not really the zombies. Something weird happened when I was out running earlier.'

Deon told Nifty about what he had experienced up on the hill during his run. Nifty listened to every detail without saying a word. No judgement, no questioning. Deon loved that about Nifty.

'Well, that must've been quite an experience.' Nifty gently touched Deon's cut hand and then noticed the blackening bruise on the side of his nephew's face. 'Did you get this on your run?'

'No.'

'At school?'

'Yeah, I copped it when Johno threw my bag at me on the bus.'

'So this happened just before you went out for a run?'

'Yeah.'

'Well, it could be the hit on the head causing a concussion. That might've made you see things.'

'It wasn't that hard a hit. And I've got grass stains on my shorts. I had fresh grass in my hand and there's no green grass up at the broken pole, it's been too dry.'

23

'It could be stress, boy genius.' Nifty shrugged. 'You've had more than enough stress and changes lately, maybe it's just a reaction to all the stuff that's been going on.'

'What, like I'm mental?' Deon blurted. 'Like I'm seeing things and hearing voices?' He stood up and shoved his hands in his pockets. 'I'd rather have a suspected concussion, Nifty. I'm not going mental.'

'Of course you're not, Deon, You're just a bit stressed. Maybe we should take a few days and go away ... fishing.'

Deon laughed out loud. 'In what alternate universe would you go fishing, Nifty? *This* is what you do to relax.' Deon waved his arms around at the dozens of gizmos in the shed. 'Would you even know where a river was around here? We couldn't fish at the beach, too many zombies.'

'I'll have you know, smarty-pants, that I used to go fishing with your dad all the time when we were young. I'll admit, I never caught a fish, but I do know where the river is.'

'Prove it, professor,' Deon teased.

'I will.' Nifty flicked through a few files on his computer and started up a slideshow of photos. They were of a young Nifty and Deon's father, sitting at the edge of a creek. There was a stepped waterfall in the background. Photo after photo flicked across the screen. Mick with a fish held high. Nifty with no fish, but holding some newly made gadget. Both boys were wearing proud, happy smiles.

'See. You were too busy making things to catch fish,' Deon teased again.

'Yeah, I think that was about when Mick started calling me Nifty.' For a long moment, he stared past the screen. Then he shook his head, sniffed and coughed.

'You two look about eight or nine years old there,' said Deon, filling the quiet. 'Where were you?'

'We were eleven and twelve, and runty.' Nifty smiled, shrugged. 'That creek is here, you know, in Moran's Cove.'

'That rock formation, I've seen it when I turn at the broken pole.'

Nifty nodded. 'Yep. Further up in the hills out west of town, where the rainforest thickens up. A place called Barnaby's Falls. We used to call it the giant's steps because there were four massive rock drop-offs making a series of smaller falls with a little pool at the bottom of each one. Right at the bottom was that fishing hole, then the creek flowed down to town and out to the sea.'

'You and Dad used to come here on holidays, but you never learned to surf while you were here?'

'I think the dislike of surfing might be genetic, boy genius. But you got your dad's fishing talent, so do you want to head up to the giant's steps in a few days and check it out?'

Deon's head filled with memories of sitting quietly with his dad for hours, waiting for the fish to bite. He leaned over, remembering nudging up against his dad's prickly fishing jumper and smiling when his dad got a bite. He gulped in a jittery sigh. 'Fishing would be great. I'll dig all the gear out of our shed.'

'In the meantime, boy genius, I need you to help me. I'm working on something and I could use an extra hand.' Nifty pointed to a partially disassembled something on the bench. 'I need you to hold it all in place for me so I can solder in a new component.' He lifted the hot soldering tool from its cradle and handed Deon some kind of circuit board. 'You line up the new piece and hold it steady, just get them touching, and I'll join them—'

Phssssht—BANG!

There was a searing white flash, some sizzling, and a cracking flare of blue flame. The flame lasted only a second, but that was long enough to lick Deon with a blast of heat. His nose twitched as the acrid smell of singed hair invaded his nostrils. He reached up and felt a crispy patch of brittle stubbly hair at his left temple.

Nifty grabbed at him protectively as the lights in the shed flickered. 'You okay, Deon?' Panic constricted his voice.

'Yeah, yeah, I'm fine.' Deon looked at Nifty and laughed.

'Oh, bugger, you look hysterical,' Nifty blurted, laughing as well. 'You have a bruise like a pirate's eye patch, and now you've been slightly exploded at. Sorry to laugh, but—'

'No, Nifty, you're the one looking hysterical. Or at least your eyebrows are.' Deon reached for a shiny metal case on the bench and held it up to Nifty's face.

Nifty's eyebrows were gone, leaving two sweaty black smudges above his eyes. Deon snorted and they both buckled across the bench laughing.

'Are you sure you'll survive a fishing trip?' Deon said, when he finally stopped laughing.

'I did when I was young,' Nifty said, smoothing down his non-existent eyebrows.

'I better get home, Mum will be wondering where I am.'

Nifty looked concerned and raised his non-eyebrows.

'Don't worry,' Deon said, 'I won't mention the … technical difficulty. Can I borrow your cap to hide the evidence?'

'Sure thing. Fishing this weekend?'

'That'll be great.' Deon smiled, shoving the cap onto his head. He left the shed and jogged toward home and dinner.

Hunch

It wasn't that far to ride to school, so Deon decided that's what he would do to avoid the bus. If he stayed out of Johno's way for a while, hopefully he could fade into social invisibility again.

'So you're riding to school,' his mother said over her morning coffee.

'Yeah, I just need a change from running for a while,' he said.

'I never thought I'd hear you say that.'

Deon never thought he'd hear himself say it, either, but he'd been thoroughly spooked by the episode up at the broken pole. The faces of the chanting weirdoes had invaded his dreams every night since the strange whatever it was had happened—or didn't. *Not Nifty, not Nifty.* It had all seemed so real.

Riding to school was a good idea—for two days. It took that long for Johno and the other zombies to clue into what

Deon was doing. On the third day, when he went to unlock his bike he found both tyres dead flat. It was a long walk, in the opposite direction to home, pushing the bike to the petrol station to pump up the tyres. After that, he decided the bus was a better option than waiting to see what they might do to his bike next, so the next two days were a blur of taunts, attempted ambushes and more brainiac-ball.

Deon handled it all with some creative invisibility, trying to ignore what he couldn't avoid, and thinking about the weekend and hiking up to the giant's steps with Nifty.

He had cobbled together a couple of rods and some fishing gear, and he decided to take it around to Nifty's shed after dinner that night. And that afternoon he would go for a run. It had been several days since he'd been up to the broken pole, and even though he still felt a bit spooked, he was hanging out for a run.

Just get over it, Deon told himself as he got changed. Nifty was probably right. It was stress, and maybe concussion. He tied his shoelaces and headed out. It felt great to stretch out into the even pace of the run, feeling the steady rhythm of his feet pounding on the road, and the thump of his heart gaining speed as he rounded the corner and pushed up the hill.

As he drew closer to his turnaround point at the pole, he felt himself pull back a bit. He was scouring the road ahead for any sign of a mirage haze, or the odd dancing light he'd seen the last time, but there was nothing. He slowed to do a U-turn around the pole and saw a glint as something caught the afternoon light.

His heart pummelled his ribs from the inside. He jumped away from the shiny object, bracing himself for … what? The push-pull, the dizziness, weird voices.

Nothing happened. He stopped. Still nothing. He bent to pick up the object and his heart flinched. The thing in his hand was a smallish square plaque, just like the ones the apparitions had worn around their necks in his hallucination. But how could it have been real?

He shoved the shiny square into his pocket and sprinted down the hill towards home. Maybe Nifty would know what the object was.

The run home had taken forever. The shower and dinner had seemed to take even longer. All Deon could think about was finding out what the mysterious object was. He could feel it inside his pocket, pressing against his leg as he sat chewing his dinner.

'Earth to Deon,' his mother sang across the table.

'Sorry, Mum, what?'

'Did you find enough fishing gear in the shed?'

'Yeah, it was a bit busted, but I fixed everything.'

'Was that hard for you, Deon?' She fidgeted with her cutlery. 'Going through things in the shed?'

'No, it was easy.' He stopped when he realised what she meant. 'No, Mum, I'm okay. It was kind of nice, looking through all Dad's stuff, remembering fun times fishing together.'

His mum reached her hand across the table and grabbed his. Her eyes were glassy. 'That's good, sweetie.' She sniffed. 'When are you and Nifty heading off?'

'I don't know yet. I'm going to drop the stuff over tonight and ask him.'

'Well, don't stay there too late, and don't forget to return his cap.' Her eyes flicked a curious look at the obvious hair malfunction caused at Nifty's. She gave Deon a questioning look that he ignored, dropping his head lower over his plate. 'How are things going at school?' she asked next.

'It's all good,' he lied.

'Have you made any friends? You haven't brought anyone home yet.'

'They all surf, Mum, so they're always at the beach.'

'Do you want to learn to surf so you fit in better?'

'I'm not sure …' He let the answer drift off.

He missed his old mates. He wasn't sure if the surf zombies had enough brain cells to take on any more friends. And, yeah, if Deon learned to surf he might fit in better, and surfing might even be fun, but it would still be the only thing he had in common with the kids at school. Deon knew that as soon as he opened his mouth to talk about anything else, that common ground would turn to quicksand. Surely he could find some way to fit in around town. He had to.

Deon concentrated on his dinner to avoid any more conversation. He could feel the corner of the square of shiny metal digging into his leg as he shifted in his chair.

With dinner, dessert and dishes finally behind him, he lifted the large pack of fishing gear onto his back, held the rods across the handlebars of his bike, and headed into the cool of early evening towards Nifty's place.

That was the other thing he had to admit was good about Moran's Cove. His mum let him roam and go for runs without a second thought. Even at night it was safe to venture out around town—as long as Johno wasn't nearby.

Nifty seemed to be the only one in town with any cares about security, with his locked shed, and the storeroom that Deon never got to see inside. Deon assumed that Nifty's security consciousness was just an old habit from when he worked on the top-secret stuff.

Deon skidded to a stop in the pool of light that spilled out the door of Nifty's shed.

'Hey, Nifty, I've got the fishing gear,' he called, swinging the pack from his shoulders and picking up the rods. 'It was all pretty busted, but I got two rods rigged up, and I found a bunch of hooks and lures. I brought everything because I wasn't sure what we'd be catching.'

Deon realised he was feeling excited, and he also realised he was talking to himself. He stepped inside the shed. 'Hey, Nifty, where are you?'

No answer.

Deon saw that the 'top-secret' storeroom was open. He decided to sneak a peek, making it look like he was searching for Nifty. He leaned around the door of the storage space. 'Hey, Nifty.' He wasn't there.

Deon sucked in a breath. The room was crammed with stuff he couldn't identify. He felt like he'd entered a spaceship. He felt the heat of guilt rising in his face as his eyes scoured the contents of the room. He was breaking the most important rule. He gripped the storeroom door, and forced himself to look away. His hands were slick with sweat as he went to push the door closed. He hesitated. 'Nifty?' His voice cracked a little. 'Nifty!'

Deon slammed the door shut. It locked with a loud click, and the security pad built into the wall buzzed and changed colour from green to the glow of stand-by orange. Deon knew Nifty would never leave the storeroom open unless he was here, so where was he? The house had been in darkness as Deon rode up the driveway, but it was normal for Nifty to lose track of time and still be working in the shed until late at night.

Deon looked around. Things were scattered over the benches, and it looked like Nifty was in the middle of something. Deon thought about how they had been 'slightly exploded' the last time he was here. Images of his dad, lying so still, flashed through his mind.

Maybe Nifty had had an accident.

Hot panic prickled through Deon's body, and he ran around checking all the places in the shed where his uncle might be lying, unseen. He was nowhere.

Not Nifty, not Nifty. His head suddenly filled with the weird chant from his alleged apparitions. *Not Nifty, not Nifty.*

Then Deon noticed the air was crackling. It was the same static he'd felt at the top of the hill, where he'd seen weird people who said weird things, and …

He remembered his hand. He ran his finger over the healing gouge that had been made by the hallucination called Link. *Sorry, mate, nothing personal … Node said to check the codes.*

Everything felt hot. Deon's brain fizzed with a theory. Although it seemed irrational, he followed his hunch anyway. He closed his eyes, took a calming breath, and tuned in with his other senses. He listened, sniffed the agitated air, and felt his skin prickle. He turned to face the source of the sputtering disturbance of static.

He opened his eyes and found himself looking through the open shed door into a swirl of shimmering light, like the haze he'd seen on the hill. This was smaller, but it definitely looked the same. In the darkness of the backyard, behind Nifty's shed where there should be no light, was a patch of what looked like pale rippling sunshine and wavering green shapes.

The rippling haze began to shrink.

On a panicked impulse, Deon ran towards the undulating haze and dived into it, bracing for a hard landing.

No Nifty

The ground wasn't where it should be. Deon was immediately tangled in the same push-pull motion he had felt on the hill, and the same static crackle. He seemed to glide through the air for a little too long. He felt the strange sensation of time slowing down, which sometimes happened when he fell over, but it was taking way too much time to get to the ground.

He landed with a thump and grabbed at the grass, hanging on until the ground stopped tilting. The grass was lush and soft against his face. There was the sweet smell of damp leaf litter. The earth smelled the way it did after a storm, but there hadn't been a storm for weeks. Not even a shower of rain. Everything around Moran's Cove had been stubble dry all summer, and Nifty was hardly a gardener.

The lushness didn't make sense. Deon breathed deeply as he did a mental check for sore spots, and any traces of injury from his landing, but he felt fine. He flipped over in the damp grass and looked around. Wherever he was, it was not Nifty's backyard, and it was no longer night time.

Cool, he thought. A portal. *Hold it together, Narnia boy, a portal equals mental.*

He lay in the grass and listened, watched. He concentrated on gathering information, trying to apply a little science theory to replace his excited portal fantasy. High humidity, unexpectedly thick vegetation … neither of these things had been present in Nifty's yard before he passed through the haze.

The sun was rising. But the sun had set only a couple of hours before. Maybe he'd knocked himself out when he bellyflopped through the …

What was that shimmering thing? And where was he?

Deon sat up and, thinking about the possibility of a concussion, he paid closer attention to how his head was feeling. There was no dizziness, and no headache. He even checked to see if maybe he'd peed his pants, because that could be a sign he'd passed out. No, he hadn't peed his pants.

It was definitely growing lighter. Time. He checked his watch. He'd left home after dinner, at about seven, and his watch was showing that it was almost eight pm, but the sky was definitely lightening. The shadows of black and grey were melting into a melange of greens. The ground where Deon sat was spongy, and he could feel the moisture from the grass and humus seeping through his clothes. He stood up and brushed off the damp twigs. He still wasn't feeling dizzy.

He was in a small clearing. He walked haltingly in a circle, looking at the tall trees that surrounded him and stretched up towards the grey blue of the early-morning sky. The forest around him was dense, and an overgrown web of thick vines hung in loops from tree to tree. Deon imagined swinging on them like Tarzan.

Tarzan? *You're hysterical, Deon.*

This place, for a million different reasons, could not be Nifty's backyard, but where was he? Could Johno and the zombies have ambushed him in the dark, knocked him out, and taken him somewhere up in the hills outside of town and dumped him? He immediately dismissed the idea as ridiculous.

Deon knew that Nifty was even more curious than he was, so it was possible his uncle wouldn't have thought to close the storeroom door before investigating the strange light—if that's what had happened. But there was no sign of Nifty here, where Deon was now. His stomach felt like he'd swallowed a brick. Nothing made sense.

When Deon had seen the shimmering in the darkness, he had acted on his hunch that Nifty had run into the haze ahead of him, and that if he followed his uncle, he would run straight into Nifty on the other side. That theory seemed irrational now, so Deon formed a new one.

Maybe there really was something wrong with him. Maybe the stupid brainiac-ball game had given him concussion without him realising it. Maybe that's what had caused his fall at the pole and the hallucinations. He wanted to wake up from this craziness. He wanted to be with his mum and Nifty in some hospital room. They could yell at him all they liked.

He closed his eyes, hoping to feel a wrench as he was whisked back to reality. Nothing happened.

Somewhere in the tangled green distance there was a cry; it sounded as though it could be human, but the sound was bouncing around the dense rainforest. Deon held his breath and listened. There it was again. It sounded like someone yelling Nifty's name. He took off at full speed in the direction of the voice.

Before he'd made it to the edge of the clearing, his foot hooked on a vine and he face planted, thudding so hard into the ground that the air was forced from his lungs. Splotches of colour danced across his vision as he struggled to calm the spasms in his diaphragm so he could draw in some air. Finally, he sucked in a hungry breath and coughed wildly. When he recovered, he realised he was lying on something sharp. It was sticking into his cheek.

He touched his face, feeling for blood, but there was none. His hand brushed against something hard, flat. He grabbed at the square, palm-sized object. It was tangled in the vines. He worked it lose and stared at it disbelievingly. It was the electronic locking pad from Nifty's top-secret storeroom.

'No way!'

Deon felt as though he had been slammed in the chest again. This was Nifty's lock, and moments ago it had been glowing orange, securely embedded in the solid wall of Nifty's solid shed. Deon's thoughts were spooling at high speed. Even if something had happened to Nifty, and even if Deon had been knocked out, how could everything have been so totally changed in such a short space of time?

Time. He looked at his watched again, then at the rising sun. Could Nifty have done something that effected time? Maybe one of his top-secret projects had done this. Who knew how many secrets Nifty still had? He'd been inventing things for decades … Deon shook his head. It wasn't just portals. Time machines equalled mental, too.

But maybe Nifty *had* invented time travel. That would explain why he kept everything so secret. This theory seemed better to Deon than the idea of being mental, so he decided to stick with it.

He strained to hear the cry again, but everything was quiet. There were no sounds at all. No, that wasn't true, they just weren't the usual Moran's Cove sounds. No cars, no kids yelling to each other, no lawnmowers.

Deon stood, and climbed up on a rotting stump to take a proper look around. He saw that the rainforest that surrounded him thinned out towards the east. Slivers of bright morning light cut through the trees. Through the gaps between the trunks, he could see that the forest transitioned, opening up to mangroves. The sun was still low, and the light was reflecting off the water that flowed between the squat mangrove trees hugging the edges of the mudflats.

Nothing he was seeing made any sense. There were mangrove flats at Moran's Cove, and the streets crept in and out between them, but Nifty's street was on the opposite side of town from the mangroves. They couldn't be this close.

Deon rubbed the angry bump on his forehead. Maybe he had become disoriented by the fall when he tripped on the vines. And time travel could cause some disorientation, he told himself ironically, in an attempt to joke away his fear.

He jumped down from the stump and scanned around more carefully. He found small traces of human habitation sprinkled through the tangled understory of the rainforest. Bent pieces of corroded metal and small sprigs of twisted wires. Not much, but they were there, hiding in the layers of green and poking out of the leaf litter.

Everything Deon found was stained and worn, as though it had been lying exposed to the weather for a very long time, but he knew that some human-made stuff could almost last forever. He picked up a few more pieces as proof that Nifty's house had once been here, in this very place. He stuffed anything that he thought might be useful into his pockets, feeling grateful for having worn his cargo pants, which gave him six oversized pockets. He didn't know what would happen next, so he had to be prepared.

He realised that he seemed to be accepting that he had travelled through time. If this *were* the future somehow, then there would be no house, he theorised. Nifty's house was made of timber and would rot away in a short space of time. But how much time?

Deon breathed fast, moving the air in and out through clenched teeth. His vision blurred as he blinked back stinging tears; crying was not helpful. He shook his head, palmed away the one tear that had escaped down his cheek, and scanned the area again.

At the edge of the clearing he saw a straight strip of ground between the trees. It was less overgrown in that direction, so he jogged through the narrow green corridor. His foot hit something hard and made an echoing, metallic clank. He looked down and saw a dented metal box attached to a corroded metal pipe. He sucked in a deep breath. Kicking the box to flip it over, he knew what he would see.

On the other side of the box was a number. It was broken, but when he pivoted the two pieces the right way it made the number eight. It was Nifty's letterbox, but it looked like it hadn't held a mail delivery for years.

Deon felt as though a boulder of confusion had landed on his shoulders. He crumpled down next to the letterbox. Then he saw the pencil. It was Nifty's pencil, or at least half of it. But it hadn't aged like the letterbox. It looked like it had just been put there.

Deon smiled. Somehow, impossibly, Nifty was also here. And if Deon knew his uncle, he had dropped the pencil to leave a trail. And If Nifty had left a trail, it meant he knew he would be followed. Before picking up the pencil, he took note of the direction it was pointing in.

The old letterbox twisted and screeched as Deon smashed it against a tree trunk. Pieces of the lid flew off in different directions. Swinging hard, Deon sank the jagged edge of the lid-less box into the bark of the tree like some weird axe. It dug in deep and stuck tight. He levered the supporting pipe back and forth until the rusty bolts finally snapped.

He was holding a solid hunk of pipe, the nearest thing he had to a weapon. 'Quark!' he said aloud. Yesterday his worst problem was the surf zombies, and the worry that they might lob a bag at his head. Today he was weaponising a letterbox.

He had a sudden thought, and grabbed hold of a sharp piece of metal from the letterbox. Now he had something that could serve as a knife.

Now what? He realised he was standing on Nifty's long-ago driveway, so he knew the direction he was facing. The strange cry had come from the south, and Nifty's pencil had been pointing the same way. South it was.

As if to reinforce his decision, there was another noise, a half-laugh, half-cry. He heard the snap of a breaking branch, also in a southerly direction. Deon took off running.

Not Dreaming

The sun continued to climb high into the sky on Deon's left as he jogged through what his wild theory had determined were the remains of a future, changed Moran's Cove. He kept his ears open for more sounds, but he chose not to look at the town too closely. He definitely did not want to recognise his own street in case he felt tempted to investigate. He was afraid of what he might discover. He knew it wouldn't help to think about what had happened, or how long ago it had happened, especially if the thoughts involved his mother.

It didn't work. The theories continued to unfold. He ran harder to push them from his mind. He refocused on listening for more crashing noises. He kept his head down and tried to ignore his surroundings, but he could not overlook one obvious thing: the ground was mushy, and everything smelled salty and silty, like the mangrove flats.

Deon was sure he had reached the centre of town, but the ground was inundated and it shouldn't have been, not this far from the shore. With creepy and ironic timing, he reached the statue of Captain Moran, the town's founder. It was rusty and weathered, and was tilted in the soggy ground like the Tower of Pisa. Deon no longer had any doubt about where he was. This was the park, near the centre of town, where there shouldn't be any mangroves; at least not in his time.

Sticking to the remains of the roads, where they had not been fully overtaken by the forest, made the going a bit easier and faster. Deon saw fragments of the old, familiar town tangled within the green: a twisted old bike wheel, a broken plastic garden chair, a faded bucket hanging impossibly high up on a tree branch.

He dropped his head again, scouring the ground for another breadcrumb from Nifty. His heart thumped out a steady comforting rhythm as he squelched through the soggy, overgrown town.

He skidded to a stop on the slippery ground. Up ahead was a freshly broken sapling, and on the ground around it was a jumble of footprints. They were human footprints, but some of the strides were enormous, with shoe-shaped impressions two or more metres apart.

'Seven league boots,' he muttered.

He spotted another piece of Nifty's pencil, pointing up the slope towards the west. The footprints also went in that direction, but then the mud ended and the prints were lost in the leaves and twigs on the forest floor.

Deon picked up the pencil and headed west, along one of the overgrown roads that led out of town. Whoever these people were, they couldn't be that far ahead. He should be able to catch up to them soon.

It was two hours since Deon had left the town. The sun was high in the sky, and although the forest gave him some protection from the sun, it was steamy under the canopy and rivers of sweat ran down his body. The salt stung his eyes, and he was starting to gross himself out with the stink that was creeping out from under his arms.

Luckily, he had seen each one of the signs that Nifty had left. Without them, Deon would have been guessing which direction to take. Sometimes there were footprints as extra clues, but most of the time he only knew he was going the right way when he found the next clue.

There had been a few tell-tale noises. He definitely heard a few more crashes, and he was sure he'd also heard laughing. Whoever he was tracking did not suspect they were being followed. That made Deon grateful; the last thing he wanted to encounter was a person with a two-metre-plus stride chasing him in crazy seven-league boots. He ran on.

Deon was exhausted. His throat burned. His stomach ached, and growled in hungry protest. He should have caught up to Nifty and the people he was with by now. Deon knew he could outrun most kids his age, and he could definitely keep pace with Nifty when they ran together. If Nifty had been taken against his will, Deon knew he would be fighting. Maybe he was refusing to walk and they were carrying him. That would slow them down. Why hadn't he been able to catch up?

He heard a distant echoing laugh and looked up. Up ahead he saw a tiny pile of wires, deliberately aligned to point south: another sign from Nifty.

Every muscle was aching, Deon had to rest for a while. He flopped to the ground and leaned against a tree, closing his eyes and listening to the erratic bursts of non-forest noises as he waited for his breathing to slow. His tongue was sticky and his throat raw. He had to find some water.

He opened his eyes and scanned for places where water might have collected. In curled leaves, maybe, or rock hollows. Then he spotted splashes of red within the green.

'No way!' He jumped to his feet and plunged towards the unbelievable sight.

Under the patchwork canopy of green gloom was a gnarled old apple tree. The apples hung from its branches on spindly stalks. They were tiny and blemished, but they were definitely apples. Deon grabbed at one and bit into it. It was sweet, and juice dripped and ran down his chin. Two more hungry bites and the apple had gone. He greedily plucked more fruit, stuffing his pockets with one hand and his mouth with the other.

As he chewed, he peered deeper into the forest and saw other choked signs of former human habitation. Beneath

46

the blanket of green were the diagonal ruins of a timber farmhouse surrounded by decaying water tanks and farm machinery. The small orchard must once have prospered on the site before whatever unexplained happening had caused the devastation of Moran's Cove.

Deon clambered deeper into the old farmyard and scrounged more food from an overgrown kitchen garden. Through a tangle of vines, he saw a tired-looking orange tree. He put on a burst of speed, intending to leap the tangle and pick the fruit, but his foot kicked into something heavy. There was a cracking, popping sound and he felt a wetness seeping into his shoe.

He froze, not game enough to look down. He thought of the roadkill he saw when he was running. What if he was ankle deep in the rotting guts of some wallaby or koala? Without looking, he carefully pulled his foot back out of the wetness. Then he smelled it. Rock melon.

He looked down and laughed. His shoe was covered in globs of sticky orange melon, and a lump of seeds and pulp was mounded up on his laces. He shook the gloop off his shoes and saw three more melons that he'd managed to miss by only centimetres. With a feast of oranges and rock melon piled in his arms he returned to the tree near Nifty's wire marker to eat.

The fruit was overripe and sweet, but the juice from the oranges quenched his thirst. He ate fast, until his hands, face and neck were dripping and sticky. He let out a long loud, fruity burp.

'Good one, Deon … and pardon me.'

Finding a shallow puddle, he managed to wash away most of the stickiness. Then he set off south again, with his full pockets jiggling like cow's udders at milking time.

Without hunger to distract him, Deon was soon thinking about Nifty again, and his thoughts started to edge towards panic. His pace slowed as he wondered if he really wanted to catch up to these people.

Whoever they were, they could time travel.

Or Nifty could time travel, and they had found him.

Or Nifty had found them and, judging by the deliberate trail Nifty had left, it looked like he was hoping to be followed and rescued.

Listen to yourself, Deon told himself. He sounded like he was travelling with Dr Who to Narnia. He had to face reality: he didn't know where he was, and he was alone.

He wished he had been nosier and asked Nifty more about the secrets he worked on. If he had, maybe he would be less clueless now about what was happening. Whoever he was chasing seemed to have unnatural speed and ease at moving through the rainforest, that was growing steadily thicker as Deon travelled up the foothills towards the escarpment to the west.

Then up ahead, through the gaps in the trees, he caught sight of glinting and movement. He slowed his pace and listened—to the quiet, normal sound of flowing, splashing water. He looked at the escarpment. It had to be the giant's steps, the waterfall that tumbled down the rocks to the forest below.

His feet slipped out from under him, and he slid off the rock he was standing on and into the creek. The water was icy. He was wet up to his knees. Teetering back and forth, he tried hard to stay on his feet, not wanting to fall in. He grabbed an overhanging vine, just managing to stay upright, and yanked hard on the vine to pull himself out.

The movement caused a grunting protest from some animal in the trees above. Deon clambered up onto the creek bank and scoured the canopy, searching for the creature. It had sounded wary and annoyed rather than angry. Deon shook his head. *What would you know about native animals, city boy?* He heard a rustling sound, but no more grunts.

He had seen no more of Nifty's breadcrumb trail for a while. The ground was uneven, and there was no way he could run now, so he decided to head for the falls. He needed water, and it would be less muddy there than here at the creek. And maybe if he could get higher up he'd be able to see something helpful.

Halfway up a jagged shelf of rock on the escarpment, Deon found a small piece of circuit board. Relief flooded through him. Nifty was still up ahead somewhere.

'I'm coming, Nifty,' he said aloud. His words echoed off the rock wall.

Above him, in the endless shady green, he could hear chittering, yowling, grunting. It sounded like the same animal from the creek. Whatever it was, maybe the escarpment was its territory. He hoped it didn't mind a visitor.

An echoing laugh came from further up the stepped falls, and the nearby animal seemed to grunt in response. Deon stood still, thinking that if he kept quiet the animal would show more interest in the laughter.

Now that he had stopped moving, he was able to take a good look at his surroundings. As lonely and strange as this place was, it was equally beautiful. Here, where craggy boulders split the forest to form the giant's steps, the air was cooler than it had been under the thick canopy. Light flooded through large gaps between the trees in golden shards.

There were more shades of green here than Deon had names for, and the air was filled with the peaty smells of the damp leaf litter that carpeted the ground below. The only sound was the constant gurgling of the water as it tumbled down over the huge rock steps, collecting in each timeworn rock pool before spilling over and flowing down the escarpment.

A gentle breeze brushed the leaves together, and there was a rustling sound high in the canopy. Deon took a deep breath. In spite of his circumstances, he started to relax.

Deep in the green shadows, the mystery animal grunted again. It was close, on his right. Then another creature made a chittering sound on his left, and again directly ahead of him. The animal on his right stopped grunting and joined in the chittering. Then it let out a piercing yowl, which was answered by a far-off noise that almost sounded like someone whistling to a farm dog.

Now the chittering was all around him. Deon stopped feeling relaxed.

There was movement in the canopy above him. The animals were closing in on him. Speckled brown shapes bustled from branch to branch until they had formed a circle around him. They gathered on the branches above his head and stared down at him. One opened its mouth, and Deon saw a bright pink tongue and a collection of very sharp teeth.

'Hi, fellas, aren't you cute,' Deon said irrationally. They weren't cute; they looked like someone had crossbred a giant possum with a guard dog.

One of the furry, spotty animals—Deon thought of them as tree-dogs—seemed to smile down at him, and then it made a noise like a cough, followed by a stretched-out yowl. The other two joined in—*ch-ch-ch-ch-ch*—and then they all howled in a three-part, toothy harmony that made Deon's blood run cold.

The howl was answered a moment later by another chirping, farm-dog whistle from further up the falls. Then the animals moved down into the lower branches of the trees. They manoeuvred around until they were slightly downstream from Deon. They opened their mouths, exposing sharp, carnivorous teeth, and hissed.

Ch-ch-ch-ch-ch, they chorused, sounding like a lawnmower that wouldn't start. They shuffled closer, moving slowly along the branches, their long claws gripping the bark. *Hsssss*. Their partly coiled tails were wagging as they came closer.

He stepped backwards until he was up against the wall of rock.

'Go on,' he growled at them, trying to bluff them into backing off, as though they *were* actual dogs. 'Get home.' Get home? They're not kelpies, he reminded himself.

The biggest tree-dog reached out a clawed paw and gripped the branch of a nearby tree, then let go with its back claws, swinging its back legs across to grip the new branch. Its tail wrapped around the branch like it had a mind of its own, and the creature dropped, hanging by its tail, above him. As it swung, Deon saw a striped underbelly that made him think of a Tasmanian tiger. This animal was making less sense by the second.

Deon scrambled up to the next level of the falls. The three tree-dogs clawed their way from branch to branch as they followed him. No, he thought, they were *herding* him. He had to stop climbing up. He had to turn around, get past them, and work his way back down the falls.

The furry trio chittered and grunted, edging closer. They took turns to hiss at him. Their breath smelled meaty, fruity. He backed into the next shelf of rock and heard a metallic clunk. He remembered the pipe he was carrying. He grabbed at it and yanked it from his belt, holding it up in the air like a club.

'Back off,' he warned, waving the pipe in the air.

The toothy fur-balls lunged, swinging at the pipe with their dangerously sharp claws.

Deon whirled the pipe above his head. The animals dodged his swings and snapped at him. He pressed his back hard into the rock and held the pipe across his face as a shield. He closed his eyes and waited for the teeth.

Drop-Bears

Claws were scraping on the rock on both sides of Deon. The teeth-filled creature was moving closer. *Ch-ch-ch-ch ch-ch.*

'That'll do, Nelly,' came a call from higher up the rocks behind Deon. The creature called Nelly made a noise that sounded like a whimper, almost like a dog begging. 'All right, but be gentle.'

Deon kept his eyes tightly closed. The animal was so close now that he could the feel the warmth of its panting, fruit-meat breath on his face. He held his own breath.

It sniffed at his hair. Then he felt the weight of the creature on his shoulder. It sniffed again and he felt the weight shift. Then he felt the claws penetrate his shirt slightly, not quite piercing his skin. It continued to sniff and move down his arm. The bristly tail coiled around Deon's neck and flicked across his face. He let out a yelp of surprise and then remembered that he had to breathe. He panted frantically.

The claws moved down his body. He felt the weight of the creature on his belt. Then he felt it nuzzling in his pocket. Those sharp teeth were in his pocket! It was probably seeking out the fruit, but it was still too close for comfort.

Deon's heart thundered, and his stomach was churning. The fruit he'd eaten was rising up into his throat. He hoped the animal wouldn't be too angry if he threw up on it.

'Hurry, Nelly, get up here.'

The head inside Deon's pocket growled.

'Now.' The voice was stronger.

The head whimpered and withdrew, and the heavy body pushed off and was gone.

'Good dog, Nelly,' the voice said affectionately. 'Good girl.'

Dog? What kind of a dog was that? Deon opened his eyes and looked up towards the voice to get an answer to his question. What he saw made the three tree-dogs look normal by comparison.

Sitting on the boulder just above Deon's head was a girl. She was patting the animal called Nelly, who was gnawing on an apple from Deon's pocket. The other two dog-like creatures sat close by. They were watching Nelly eat, and whimpering enviously.

'Do you have any more apples?' the girl called down to him.

Deon looked up at her. She looked about the same age as him, but everything else was dissimilar—in a very strange way. She was wearing something that looked like a Lycra bike outfit: tight shorts and a zipped-up shirt made out of a stretchy green fabric, and it looked like she was carrying—no, wearing—a metal frame. The frame was made up of a series of slim rods that ran down the outside of her arms and legs. The rods seemed to be attached to her clothing with small plates of metal. The rods were hinged so the girl could bend her arms and legs, and she seemed to be sitting with ease, as though the frame wasn't there.

Now Deon had another strange thing to add to his growing collection of strange things.

Then he saw something that did look familiar. The girl was wearing the same necklace that he had seen in his hallucination-dream episode. He counted seven shiny palm-sized squares hanging from what looked like a twisted cable around her neck.

He slipped his hand into his leg pocket and touched the black square he'd found near the pole, the object he had wanted to show Nifty … yesterday? Or was it earlier today? He was thoroughly confused. He shivered.

'I hope you've got more,' the girl said.

Deon felt his face heat up. He feared she could somehow tell what he was touching. 'More what?' he stammered.

'More fruit, Rex and Cuddlepie get a bit mean if you play favourites.'

He looked at the sharp, carnivorous teeth. 'These things don't look like they eat fruit.' It felt beyond strange to be talking about pet food at a time like this.

'Well, they do, but they'll eat anything, trust me on that.' The girl gave a menacing smile.

'Right.' Deon pulled two more apples out of his pocket.

The creatures called Rex and Cuddlepie jumped forward, leaning over the rock ledge. Deon shrank back, dropping the apples.

'Stop!' the girl commanded, and her pets froze. 'Drop.' They settled down onto their clawed haunches and whimpered. She reached down, and Deon slowly retrieved the apples and passed them up to her.

'Say please,' she said, holding the apples in front of her pets. The creatures yowled a discordant tune and she lofted the fruit. They jumped, caught the apples with their dagger teeth, and settled down to munch.

'What's your name?' she asked.

'Deon,' he rasped, keeping an eye on the munching pets.

'You following us?'

'Well, yeah. Well, no. I was looking for my uncle … Nifty.'

'No uncles around here, just me and the drop-bears.'

'*Us* and the drop-bears,' said another voice behind the girl.

Deon saw two boys appear. They all seemed to be about his own age. Each wore the same type of metal frame and necklace as well. This was more than enough strangeness for Deon. His legs buckled. He sat down hard against the rock, and breathed even harder.

'Hey, are you okay?' one of the new arrivals said, as he jumped off the rock ledge and sat down beside Deon.

Deon's head was spinning. He tried to slow his breathing.

'He looks freaked out—over,' the other boy said.

'Shut up, Bump,' the first boy said.

'Just sayin' it like I see it—over and out.'

56

'You all right, mate?' asked the first boy, who had dark shaggy hair. 'My name's Scout.' He held out his hand.

Deon reached to shake it, expecting it to disappear when he touched it. It all had it be some kind of dream. 'Hi.' The hand was real. 'I'm Deon. What's going on? Where am I?'

'I'm Bump—over.' The other boy's hand appeared.

Deon shook it. 'Hi,' he mumbled, staring at the hand closely. He could feel the rods attached to the hand. The metal frames were as real as the hands he was shaking. He could swear that the hardware was somehow attached to the skin.

'You've already met Glide and her quollagoes,' Scout said.

'Who? And the what?'

'Glide.' Scout pointed to the girl. She leaned over and waved. 'And the drop-bears.'

'Drop-bears?'

'Well, they partly are, and they often do,' Scout said. 'Drop, that is.'

Deon shrugged and shook his head. Asking questions wasn't helping. The answers he was getting were only making things more confusing.

'They're not drop-bears, they're hybrids.' Glide patted her pets proudly. 'They're quoll, koala and dingo, a blend of the last marsupials. It was the only way to save them from being gone for good.'

'Not now, Glide.' Scout took hold Deon's arm. 'Are you okay to stand?'

'Upsy-daisy—over.' The kid called Bump jumped down and took Deon's other arm, and the two boys hefted him to his feet. They pushed him up onto the next level with no effort at all, which surprised him.

He landed next to Nelly, who immediately started nuzzling his pockets for more food. He pulled all the fruit out of his pockets and threw it across the rocks. The tree-dogs scampered after it and left him alone. Deon wasn't quite ready to call them 'quollagoes' yet.

'Look, I'm just trying to find my uncle,' he said.

'Nifty?' Glide flicked a strange look at Scout, who shrugged. Bump opened his mouth to speak.

'Over and out, Bump,' Glide snapped, and glared at him.

'Over and out.' Bump sat down in a sulk and closed his eyes.

'So, when did you last see your uncle Nifty?' Glide asked.

'A couple of days ago, and then I went to his house last night, or this morning, I don't know when it was, and there was this weird light.'

'What do you mean, weird light?' Scout said.

'I don't know. It was like a mirage—light where there shouldn't be light. I saw it last week, too.'

'What time of day did you see it for the first time?'

'It was afternoon, when I was out running, but it was night on the other side.'

'The other side of what?' asked Glide.

'I don't know.' Deon jammed his clenched his fists into his pockets. 'I don't know anything.' He felt the smooth square in his pocket.

'It could all have been a dream,' said Glide.

'Well, is this a dream?' He pointed to the black necklaces they all wore. 'I saw people wearing those.'

'Dreams are funny things, Deon,' said Scout.

'That's not good enough, tell me what's going on.' Deon pulled the square piece of necklace out of his pocket and held it up. It fitted perfectly into the gap on Scout's necklace.

'My lost power cell, thanks.' Scout took the black square and raised his eyebrows in Glide's direction.

'I found that piece where I'd seen the haze and the weirdness last week,' Deon said. 'I want to know where Nifty is. I went to his house last night … well, whenever it was, and the shed was all lit up and unlocked. I wanted to show it to him, but he wasn't there. I saw the shimmering light thing again. I jumped at the haze and ended up … I don't know where. Here, where everything is changed and gone. Then I followed Nifty's trail of pencils and wires.' He pulled Nifty's breadcrumb trail out of his pockets to show them.

Now Glide's eyebrows were raised, and she looked serious. 'Well, you don't see your uncle with us, do you?' She shrugged and looked at the ground.

'But I heard you guys when I was running through the forest,' Deon said. 'And Nifty left this trail. I followed it and it led me to you.'

'It led you here, Deon,' Glide said gently, 'but maybe your uncle is hiding.'

'This forest is a big place, mate,' said Scout. 'There are plenty of places to hide.'

'Nifty wouldn't hide from me, not Nifty.'

'Not Nifty, not Nifty,' came a mumble from Bump, who seemed to be asleep.

'Over and out,' Glide growled towards the dozing Bump. Then she forced a smile. 'Don't mind Bump. The installation of his augz didn't go quite right, so he's a little different from the rest of us.'

'Augz?'

'Augmentations.' Glide held out her arms. 'These things are add-ons. They make us stronger, faster.'

'Better, stronger, faster,' echoed the sleeping Bump. 'We have the technology—over.'

'Over and out, Bump,' Glide said again.

'None of this is making any sense.' Deon felt as if his brain would explode. Every time he asked a question, all he got were more questions and weirdness. 'What is all this? Where am I? What was the shimmering light? Where's Nifty?'

There was a piercing whistle from further up the escarpment. Glide and Scout both turned to listen. There was a second whistle. They nodded to each other.

'That's our muster signal,' Glide said. 'We've got to go.'

Deon's shoulders sagged.

'Come with us,' Scout said.

'But I can't,' Deon protested. 'I have to find my uncle.'

'You can't be out here on your own after dark,' Glide said.

Deon looked around and noticed the sun was dipping towards the west. She was right.

'Come with us and rest,' Scout said. 'Get some food and some information.'

Deon looked around at the tall trees, the cragged rocks and the darkening sky. They were right. He was bone weary. 'Thanks.'

'Bump,' called Scout. 'Ready to go?'

'Always ready—over.' Bump sprang clumsily to his feet. Then he picked up a large bundle, and climbed up and out of sight.

'Hop on,' Scout said to Deon, tapping his shoulder and offering a piggyback ride.

Deon looked sceptical. 'Really?'

Scout nodded. 'It'll be faster.'

Glide gave three sharp, distinct whistles, and Nelly, Rex and Cuddlepie scampered up. 'Go home, babies,' she said. The three animals shot up the tree trunks and darted through the canopy.

Glide clambered onto a rocky outcrop and sprang into the air. She opened a wide set of wings and glided out of sight.

Deon gasped. 'What …'

'A few bounces and you'll have all the answers you're looking for,' Scout said. He was springing up and down where he stood, and Deon could hear the metal framework hissing. 'Hop on.' Scout smiled and gestured over his shoulder again.

Deon jumped onto Scout's back, and had barely got a grip before he was jolted upwards through a blur of green. His teeth clanged together with each bouncing step Scout took. He struggled to focus as his head rattled. He heard shouts and laughter, then a crash, and he saw Bump crumple to the ground in a clumsy heap. Then Bump got up and bounced away again.

Glide reappeared for a moment then vanished into the green as Scout jostled him higher up the falls and into the rainforest.

North Bower

Seven-league boots, Deon thought, as he clung to Scout's shoulders. He listened to the augz hiss as Scout sped through the blur of green, dodging trees and leaping over rocks.

They stopped at the bottom of a giant tree trunk. 'Hang on,' Scout said, and started up the tree as easily as if he was climbing a ladder.

When they were high in the branches, everything tilted. Deon gasped at the sight of the ground so far below him, and clung on tighter. The world started to right itself when Scout climbed over a railing and dropped down onto a wide platform.

'Welcome to North Bower,' Scout said, stepping away from the edge.

Deon slid ungracefully from Scout's back and wobbled over to the railing. He looked out across the dense green valley. Beyond the valley, he caught a glimpse of the coast and the place where Moran's Cove should have been.

'Where are we? What is this place? Where are all the ... normal people?'

He looked around, trying to comprehend everything he was seeing. He walked towards the centre of the circular treetop platform, which was built into the spreading branches of the massive tree. He wobbled and leaned against the smooth bark of the trunk to steady himself.

After a moment, he walked back towards the railing and the edge of the enormous treehouse platform. He leaned over the wooden rail. The platform was well disguised among the cover of leaves and vines that formed a crisscross tangle in the narrow valley.

'There's no way anyone could see this platform from the ground,' said Deon.

'Can't see it from the air, either,' said Scout. 'We're well hidden here in the canopy. We have to be.' Before Deon could ask why, Scout pointed across the cascading falls that roiled and sparkled far below, and towards the trees on the other side. Deon looked hard in the direction he indicated and could now see another platform on the other side of the creek, camouflaged by thick leaves and the same vines that were entwined in all the other trees.

'Very impressive.'

'Thanks.'

'So how do you get to the other side? Swing on the vines?'

'They're not all vines. Some of them are polymer cables,' Scout said. 'The flyers can just glide across, but the rest of us use zip-lines to move between bowers.'

'Flyers?'

'Well, referring to your previous question regarding "normal" people …' Scout raised his eyebrows.

'Sorry,' said Deon.

'There are the Havz, that's us. We have augz, augmentation.' Scout lifted his arms and did a slow turn, showing the metal exoskeleton running along his arms and legs. The rods were connected across his body with thin metal strapping that flexed as he moved.

'High tech.' Deon puffed out a breath.

'Thanks. I'm a bouncer, we're good at moving across rough terrain.'

'I know, what a wild ride that was.'

'You're welcome.' Scout pointed out across the treetops. 'Here comes Glide, she's a flyer. Depending on power supply and weather conditions, flyers can cover long distances. They can manoeuvre through and under the canopy, and travel through the deep forest unnoticed.'

A set of wings appeared out of the darkening sky as Glide approached the tree, making Deon think of a bat crossing the evening sky. When she reached the platform, she folded her wings and made a graceful landing on the railing. Then she jumped down onto the deck.

'Incredible,' Deon gasped.

'Thank you.' Glide took a bow.

'Deon's wondering where the normal people are,' said Scout.

'I didn't mean it that way.' Deon felt his face heat up.

'Around here it's just the Havz and the Notz,' said Glide. 'I guess you could say that as far as people go, we're the new kind of normal. At least we have more humanity than the Notz.'

'Nots?'

'The Notz, N-o-t-z,' she explained. 'They're the people that are *not* doing the augmentation. They don't believe in it. They believe that our augz make us robots, and not humans anymore.'

'So where are the Notz?'

'Not here, get it?' Glide laughed at her own joke. 'And they're not as interesting as us.'

Deon laughed along, but his head pounded as he tried to make sense of this frightening and frustrating day. 'Scout showed me his augz, but that doesn't help me understand.' He shook his head. He felt like he was a lost pre-schooler who'd strayed into a foreign-language maths class. He had no hope of getting any of this figured out, and that was a new and unfamiliar feeling for him.

'Hey, it's day one, you'll catch on,' Scout said, 'give yourself some time.'

'What do you mean, give myself some time? I came here to find Nifty, that's all. And when I do we're heading home.' Deon's stomach clenched with fresh fear. His task felt impossible right now.

'We know you're scared for your uncle.' Scout shot Glide a strained look. 'Do we have anything to tell Deon about his uncle?'

'I did a check.' Glide glared at Scout and ruffled her wings. 'We cannot say that we've seen your uncle Nifty … but there's been no sighting of any Notz action anywhere in the area, and no sign of anyone wandering lost, either.'

'See, no sign of your uncle,' Scout said to Deon.

'But there's no sign of anything. Moran's Cove is gone. The sea has flooded the town.' Deon stabbed his finger in the direction of the place that, up until today, was home. 'I know I was at Nifty's when I saw the haze and dived in and whatever it was happened. That's when everything stopped making sense. And I'm sure the stuff I found was a trail left by Nifty.'

'Maybe your uncle has set up camp for the night.' Glide raised an eyebrow. She glanced at Scout and shrugged. 'We might be able to send out a couple of flyers to search for any sign of a campfire.'

'But I don't get it,' Deon said. 'How can Nifty or I even *be* here? Help me understand all this.' He ran his hands through his tangled, grimy hair.

'First we need to figure out what happened to you,' said Glide. 'If you travelled here somehow, we need to investigate that. I'll get Fuse to search the plexus and look for some kind of answer. Maybe someone's done some experiments in the area we don't know about yet.'

The kid called Bump appeared. He walked down a staircase that Deon hadn't noticed and stepped onto the platform. 'Node will know—over,' Bump said, and flopped down onto a shaggy-looking sofa.

'Fuse is out with Link,' said Scout. 'They went out yesterday with the others to collect data from the gauges. They'll be back in the morning, so your search for information will have to wait until then.'

'Link!' Deon blurted. 'Did you say Link? Who's that?'

Scout and Glide stared at each other for a long moment. Glide shook her head minutely.

'Link's one of our team,' said Scout, too loudly. 'I told you all about him before. That's why you know the name. He works with data and communication. He can connect to the plexus.'

'Connect to Node—over,' added Bump.

'No, I met him,' Deon insisted. 'He was there when I went through the first time. He introduced himself.' Deon held up his hand. 'He scratched me, then apologised, saying something about codes.'

Glide took Deon's hand and looked at his palm. 'It could just be a cut from the power cell you had in your pocket, they're really sharp. Your memory's probably messed up because you're so worried about your uncle. How about I send a request to South Bower and see if we can send out some flyers?'

'What about the ...' Deon began, before glancing out over the trees. The sun had set, and he thought about Nifty, possibly alone out there in the blackness of the forest. Everything he was about to say vaporised from his mind and instead he just nodded. 'Thanks.'

'For now, how about a shower, which you really need, by the way, and dinner.' Glide wrinkled her nose.

'But—'

'After dinner, there'll be time for questions,' Scout added. 'Right now you stink, mate. Let's go up and I'll show you the showers and the sleeping rooms.'

Deon realised he didn't have the mental energy to keep asking questions. He needed food and rest before he tried to work it all out—if he even could. He nodded and followed Scout up the narrow staircase that wrapped around the trunk of the tree.

The level above the main platform was smaller and more enclosed. Scout led Deon to a small room that looked out across the dark forest. The moon was full and rising, spreading a glitter of light over the treetops. The forest sloped down towards the coast, and beyond the trees was the dark expanse of the sea. It reflected the moonlight in random, tumbling glints as the waves rolled in across the ocean. Deon took a deep breath, surprised at the beauty of the scene.

'Stunning, hey?' Scout said quietly. 'I forget how amazing it looks when you're seeing it from up here for the first time.'

'So how long have you been here? Where are you all from?'

'Just enjoy the view,' Scout said, 'the questions can wait. And you stink, remember?' He led Deon to a room with several shower cubicles and shoved a bundle of clothes at him. 'Lose the stink and put these on. I'll see you downstairs when you're done.' He turned and disappeared into one of the other showers.

Robot Night

Returning to the main level of the bower, Deon felt clean, but self-conscious. He was dressed in what looked like tightfitting bike pants. He didn't go swimming much, but he felt exposed, like he was wearing Speedos instead of the usual board shorts. These pants were like a hybrid between Speedos and board shorts. He pulled at the front of his shirt to make it sit lower.

Scout, Glide and Bump were wearing the same outfits, but without the self-consciousness. They were sitting around a wooden table, talking earnestly.

'Company—over,' said Bump, as Deon reached the bottom of the stairs. The others fell silent.

'Come on over, it's getting cold,' chirped Glide. 'Bean casserole, salad and garlic bread, dig in.'

Deon smelt the garlic and his empty stomach groaned. He was relieved to find that in the future, food didn't come in tubes filled with gloop made from something mysterious and gross. As he sat down he noticed that none of the other three had the metal rods on their arms and legs anymore. 'Wow, you look norm … different.'

'We don't wear the augz at home,' Glide said.

'So you live here?' Deon asked as he heaped food onto his plate.

'Sure do—over,' Bump said.

'Where are your parents?'

Glide smiled. 'That's a long story that can wait. I'm sure you have better questions to ask than that.'

'Nifty?' he asked around a mouthful of food.

'Can't say we've got anything we can tell you about him yet,' said Glide.

'Can't tell you yet—over.'

'Keep chewing, Bump,' said Scout. Bump turned his attention back to his plate.

'Bump's a bit unique,' said Glide quietly, 'but all us Havz stick together, regardless of how the installation of our augz turns out.'

'You can't get it reversed?' Deon asked.

'Not an option,' Scout said. 'And even if it was, no one would want to.'

'Tell me about that.' Deon he reached out slowly to touch the metal patch on Scout's arm.

'Okay, big questions first,' Scout said. 'Let's give him the snack-sized version of augmentation information or we'll be here all night.'

'Snack-sized—over.' Bump reached for more bread.

'These squares on our arms and legs,' Glide said, touching the patch of flexible metal on her arm, 'are attached to our bones. They also house a connection to our nervous system so we can control our movements when we're wearing the augz.'

'As you can imagine,' Scout added, 'it's a pretty intricate installation process. It rarely goes wrong, but if it does'—he subtly pointed in Bump's direction—'we make the most of it.'

'The structures behind the plates wrap around bone,' Glide continued. 'When the frames are in place, they anchor to the plates and are held there by strong magnets in the frame. Within the joiner plate there's a plex connection. Sorry, plex is a sort of wire that conducts electrical signals from our nervous systems so we can make the augz move. The frames run on solar power. The necklace is an array of PV panels and a storage cell.'

PV: photovoltaic panels. Finally Deon had heard something he understood. 'I've read about exoskeletons before, but I've never heard of any attaching directly to the user's bones. That's a huge leap from where we …' Deon's head spun as his tried to accept what he was hearing.

'What's up?' said Scout.

'What year is this?'

'Warm plus two-seven-five—over,' Bump said.

'Is that a Bump thing?' queried Deon.

'No, that's how we express the year. It means two hundred and seventy-five years after the no-return point,' said Scout. 'They used this dating system before we came along. That was the year when the scientists knew there would be no turning back. There was nothing humans could do to reverse climate change. The atmosphere was going to stay warmed. The damage was done, and things could only continue to get worse. It'll take a long time to undo the damage. The Tellings say that things got pretty chaotic with the storms and inundations. Lots of places and records on the planet were destroyed.'

'Women and children first—over.'

'And people, too.' Glide patted Bump's shoulder.

'I remember the warnings about a point of no return,' Deon said. 'Scientists predicted that it would happen in two thousand and fifty. So that means the Moran's Cove that I was in yesterday existed over three hundred years ago.' Deon's skin prickled.

'Today Is tomorrow when it's yesterday—over.'

'Warming and flooding would explain the way Moran's Cove looks,' Deon said. 'But what's the explanation for how I got here, to this alleged future? Maybe Nifty was working on some time-travel thing. He had lots of projects on the go that he wouldn't let anyone see, and that weird hazy light patch was in his backyard. Then I dived in and had a feeling of being pulled and stretched. Then I was dumped on the ground.' He shuddered.

'Scooped—over.'

'Bump!' snapped Glide. 'Hey, that's a good idea. Go scoop some ice cream.'

'Ice cream—over.'

Deon watched Bump walk around the stairs and enter what seemed to be the kitchen. 'You have ice cream in the future?'

'Well, it's creamy and it's cold, but … well, explaining things about food is a bit complicated,' said Scout.

'More complicated than augmentation and a new way of recording time?'

There was a chiming sound from somewhere beyond where they were sitting.

'Mail call,' said Scout.

Glide stood up. 'I'll check the bucket.'

'Bucket?' asked Deon.

'Low-tech message system between the bowers for when there's no one to link to the plexus.'

'Right. Glad I asked.'

'It's delicious—over.' Bump plonked a bowl in front of Deon. It was full to overflowing with cold, sweet-smelling blobs.

While Deon ate, Glide and Scout continued to theorise about how he got to this place—or rather, time.

'There's been no sign of campfires or tracks that might be your uncle or anyone else,' Glide said. 'Maybe he made this travel thing happen from his end and—'

'Scooped—over.'

'Shush, Bump,' Glide growled. 'Go wash the bowls.'

'Maybe you got caught up in all of that somehow and that's how you ended up here,' said Scout. 'We'll try and find out tomorrow. When Link and Fuse get back we can search the plexus.'

'Is the plexus like the web?' Deon said. 'Could I do that? I'm always searching online.'

'Going online is not quite that simple anymore, but we'll do it as soon as the others get back.'

'It's robot night—over.' Bump pointed to the moon.

'Yeah, Bump, all right, it's robot night,' said Glide. She walked over to the circle of low couches, pushed a button in the table, and a screen rolled down from the ceiling.

'Every full moon we have a bit of a ritual.' Scout waved Deon over to the couch. 'We watch ancient vid fragments showing what people back in the past thought robots would be like. No one guessed robots would look like … us.'

'Augmented bio-forms.' Glide corrected him with a smile. 'Klaatu barada nikto—over.'

Deon smiled. *'The Day the Earth Stood Still,'* he said.

'Ah, he's one of us,' Scout said, laughing.

'That movie was old even for me.' Deon let himself laugh, too, and for a while his thoughts about Nifty faded. His head was filled with the images that flashed up on the screen. Gort, guarding the space ship in *The Day the Earth Stood Still*; *Astro Boy*; Data; *WALL-E*; Marvin, the paranoid android from *The Hitchhiker's Guide to the Galaxy*; the various terminators; Robby from *Forbidden Planet*; C-3PO and BB-8 from the *Star Wars* movies; even Optimus Prime from the Transformers franchise.

The moon was high in the sky and flooded Deon's small sleeping chamber with cool light. In the bower, everyone slept in hammocks. Deon could feel the gentle swaying as his hammock rocked, responding to the slight movements of the huge tree. He had almost forgotten they were in a tree. He smiled, imagining how amazingly cool it would be to be up here in a storm. As he rocked, he watched the leafy patches of moonlight and shadow patterning the walls.

Somewhere in the quiet darkness, he heard Bump mumble in his sleep: 'I'll be back.' Deon waited to hear the word 'over', but it didn't happen.

It was hard for Deon to remember a time when he felt more tired than today, even after the half-marathon he'd run before he left the city. His muscles were sore from the day's exertions, but maybe some of it was from all the laughing. He hadn't laughed that much since he'd moved to Moran's Cove.

He really did feel like he was 'one of them', like Scout had said. They were good people, Scout, Glide and Bump. Massively odd, but so had everything else been today. It was important to them that they stuck together, stood by each other. Deon admired that. It had been like that for him, too, with his old mates back in the city.

Maybe Nifty wasn't here. He could be safe at home right now. Deon couldn't lose Nifty. 'Not now that Dad's gone,' he whispered. If he could just convince himself that Nifty was safe, he could handle the challenge of getting back home.

He looked up. The stars looked the same in the future. He drifted into sleep.

Huggy Dance

Morning light slanted through the gaps between the branches, and painted bright splotches across the floor and walls of the bower.

Deon reached the bottom of the stairs and saw Scout leaning against the railing. 'Good morning.'

'Good morning—over,' said Bump from the kitchen.

'Morning, Deon,' said Scout, 'you hungry? Breakfast won't be long.'

Deon was hungry, and whatever breakfast was smelled great. 'While I was watching the sun rise and trying not to think about Nifty, I went over the things you and Glide were saying last night and came up with a couple of theories.'

'You must've slept well,' Scout said. 'Okay, theorise away.'

'This plexus that makes your augz work, it must bond to the organic structures in the body, kind of like a network of interlacing nerves. There are similar structures in the body.'

'Plexus, Latin meaning plaited, interwoven—over.'

'Nice one, Bump,' said Scout.

'I've seen your augz working,' Deon continued. 'Whoever invented them did a good job of melding machine to body, so they must be able to work the other way to create some kind of organic connection that works the other way to connect to your version of the internet, right? So is that what they've done here?'

'The boy genius knows his stuff.'

'Yeah, I'm a real brainiac.' When Scout gave him a strange look, he added, 'It's just a name that some kids at school call me.' Deon explained about Johno and his henchmen, but Scout's odd look remained. 'What did I say?'

'I'm just a bit surprised to hear you use the term brainiac.'

'Why?'

Scout didn't get a chance to answer. Glide swooped in over the railing and crumpled onto the floor with a total lack of the grace she had shown the day before.

'I just came from Node,' she told Scout. 'Fuse and Link have been taken. They messaged that the Notz have them. Before they stopped signalling, they said they were being taken to the station at End of the Line.'

'How could that happen?' Scout started pacing. 'They were with Retro and Throttle, who would've just bounced Fuse and Link away from the Notz.'

Glide shrugged and shook her head. 'I don't know the details, but the Notz somehow got Retro and Throttle out of their frames and mangled them, nabbed Fuse and Link, and took off. Retro wouldn't leave Throttle alone to follow them.'

'Throttle's a no-go—over.'

'Too right, Bump,' Glide said. 'We'll need the back-up frames or Throttle isn't going anywhere under his own power.'

'What about Nifty?' An acidic panic rose inside Deon. 'These Notz, do they have Nifty, too?'

'They don't have Nifty,' Glide snapped. 'We're going to need you to come with us, Deon. If they get to End of the Line before we catch up to them, it'll be easier to get inside the station building with you helping.'

Scout looked at Deon. 'You don't have any augz, do you, Deon?'

'What a stupid question, how could I have augz?'

Glide shot a laser-beam look at Scout.

'And there it is again,' Deon said, 'another one of those looks. I saw you guys exchanging looks like that last night. Add that to the dilated pupils, which means your brains are working hard to make up stories, and the micro facial gestures that mean you're trying too hard to look calm when you're not. What are you two lying to me about?'

'He's good—over.'

'Are you sure you don't have anything installed?' Scout asked Deon, smiling.

'Just this.' Deon tapped his head. Regardless of the frustration of these conversations, he felt a sense of belonging that he hadn't felt since he'd left the city. With Scout and Glide, being smart was a good thing. 'Now tell me what you're holding back or I won't help you wash the breakfast dishes, let alone volunteer for some rescue mission.'

'We're not—' Glide started.

'Link was there when this happened.' Deon touched the healing scratch on his hand. 'He must know things about Nifty, and I need to find out what they are. What if …' He took a deep gulp of air and tried hard stop his legs from turning to jelly. Wobbling to the table, he sat down heavily. He rested his head in his hands. Tears of frustration and fear were stinging his eyes.

'We've found Nifty.' Glide sat down beside Deon and put her hand on his shoulder. 'He's fine.'

Deon let out a long, shuddering breath into his hands. He knew it sounded like a sob, but he didn't try to hide it. 'Where is he?' He wiped away a vagrant tear as he sat up.

'He was recovered, and he spent the night with Node.'

'Node?'

'Node is a … sort of information-storage centre.' Glide shot another look at Scout, and he nodded in response.

Deon realised they weren't trying to hide that they were hiding things from him now.

'They, I mean Nifty, spent time exchanging information with Node. He's fine, but he's sleeping now. He was exhausted.' Glide grabbed Deon's hand. 'Deon, we really could use your help on this recovery.'

'I want proof that Nifty's here and that he's okay before I do anything.'

'Fine. Nifty asked for a message to be passed onto you. It's weird, but here goes. *How about a huggy dance?* Mean anything to you?'

Deon didn't know whether to laugh or cry. He chose to laugh. 'When can I see him?'

'He really is sleeping, and we need you. Please,' Glide asked.

Deon could see how worried they were about Link and Fuse, and the others, and he knew exactly how that felt. 'I'm happy to help, but seeing as I don't fly or bounce, how helpful can I be?'

'Breakfast is ready—over.'

'They found my uncle,' Deon said to Bump, just to hear himself say the words.

'Nifty's with Node—over.'

'How did Bump know that?' Deon scowled at Glide.

'He's not deaf,' she stammered. 'He heard us talking.'

'Let's plan while we eat,' said Scout, putting plates of food on the table. 'Fast.'

While Deon chewed through fruit salad, eggs and seedy bread, and drank something that tasted like hot Milo, even though he couldn't imagine how Milo could have survived into the future, Glide and Scout explained why the rescue would be much easier with him along.

'You have no augz, Deon,' Glide said, 'which means that, essentially, you're one of the Notz. Their security system is set up to detect us and our augz, but you have nothing on board that will set off their sensors.'

Deon nodded. 'So what's the deal with these Notz?'

'The Notz chose to shun the idea of the biotech,' Scout explained. 'They mostly live in the cities, further inland, where it's easier to ignore all the things they're responsible for out here. They choose not to have augmentation, and they hate us for having it. We use the advantage the augz gives us to try and fix the things the Notz have done.'

'The warming and the floods?' asked Deon.

'Yeah,' said Scout. 'And other stuff that's much worse.'

'They hate the idea of augz,' Glide interjected before Scout could go into detail, 'but they like having access to the plexus. And they need brainiacs to get a connection.'

'Brainiacs?' questioned Deon. 'Weird to hear that word … my word has lasted into the future.'

'Yeah,' said Scout. 'Strange coincidence.'

'So these Notz kidnapped Fuse and Link because they can give them the connectivity they need.' Deon flexed his injured palm and remembered the way Link had zoned out and mumbled. 'So Link has augz that allow him to connect with this plexus?'

'Yeah, him and Fuse and other brainiacs.'

Deon looked at the metal patches in Scout's flesh and shuddered. 'Sounds … invasive.'

'It's a straightforward process when they're here connecting through Node, but it's not pretty the way the Notz have to do it,' said Scout.

'And it's a long story that'll have to wait,' said Glide. 'We've got to get to End of the Line before they put Fuse and Link on the train.'

Blue Ring

Bump, have you got those two frames packed?' Glide shouted as she stowed a spare set of wings into a small pack on her chest.

'All present and accounted for—over.' Bump shrugged a large pack onto his back.

'How did Retro and Throttle lose their augz?' asked Deon.

'Not sure yet,' said Glide.

'Why didn't they just follow on foot?'

'There's no way Retro would've left Throttle immobile.'

'Immobile?'

'Later,' Scout said, patting his shoulder. 'We've got to go now. Come on, up you get.' Deon climbed up onto Scout's back, and Scout wrapped a strap harness around them both. 'We wouldn't want to lose our secret weapon now, would we?' He shot Deon a grin over his shoulder.

'Moving out—over,' Bump called. He hitched himself to the zip-line and flashed across to the tree on the other side of the waterfall.

Glide sprang into the air from the railing. She circled the tree, and then flapped her wings and lifted up over the canopy, swooping away towards the south.

Scout bounded to the edge of the bower, and Deon heard a *click* as he attached to the zip-line, and then a *zing* as they rushed along the cable. It had been nearly dark when they'd arrived the night before, and visibility had been limited, so as they crossed between the two bowers he took the opportunity to play tourist. The trees at the top of the cliff hid the source of the waterfall, but he could see the water cascading downwards from one massive rock step to the next. The water fizzed over the edge of each step and splattered into the pool below, each of which had been formed by thousands of years of pounding water.

In seconds they had reached the other side. Scout unclipped from the zip-line, and then everything speeded up. Scout swung from the thick branch that held the cable, and they landed heavily against the trunk of the giant tree that supported South Bower. Everything was suddenly inverted and they started plummeting headfirst down the trunk. Deon gasped and clung on tight as Scout scuttled down the tree like some crazy, bionic goanna.

In moments they were on the ground and upright again, but before Deon could ask Scout to warn him next time, Scout made an abrupt change in direction, and the bouncing began.

Under the thick forest canopy, Deon no longer use the sky and the ground to orient himself. All he saw, when he managed to look over Scout's shoulder, was light green, dark green, light green, dark green, olive green, emerald green, teal, turquoise … endless blurs of every shade of green. He tried to name each colour as they rushed past his addled vision, hoping he could distract his stomach. He swallowed hard to push his breakfast, which was now bubbling and rising up his oesophagus, back down to his stomach.

Just when Deon had started to see the speeding foliage as normal, and gain control of his stomach, he heard a laughing call from somewhere behind them.

'Hop, skip and jump—over,' Bump yelled, and went sailing up over their heads. He landed ahead of them, and sprang into the green blur.

'Bump got me!' Scout laughed and increased speed.

Within a few bounds, Deon could see glimpses of Bump up ahead. As soon as he was close enough to Bump, Scout launched himself into the air and leapt over him. Now Deon's oesophagus felt like it had become a rollercoaster track for his breakfast. Scout landed with a tooth-crunching shudder and sprinted away. Within moments, Bump was laughing and galloping up behind them.

Then there was a crash in the trees to their right.

Bump laughed. 'Poor outcome—over.'

Deon could hear branches breaking, and recognised the strange laughing and crashing sounds he had heard the day before.

Without warning, Glide appeared through a gap in the trees. She flapped down to the ground front of them. When Scout had slowed and stopped, she asked him,

'Is Bump all right?' She gestured towards the noise in the underbrush.

Scout shrugged. 'He always is.'

'What was that all about?' Deon asked Scout.

'Just a friendly game of leapfrog,' Scout said. 'Bump always loses, and then he always starts another game. It's a Bump thing.'

'Come here, Bump,' Glide called, 'and let me check your load.'

Bump's face appeared out of the green, then disappeared as he tripped over a vine and face planted. 'I'm fine, load's fine—over.'

'I'll check anyway.' Glide brushed the leaves out of Bump's hair, smiled at him and checked his backpack. 'Retro and Throttle are just up ahead,' she told Scout, 'maybe a kilometre. They look fine except for the obvious.'

Scout checked something that looked to Deon like a watch, but then he realised it was some kind of tracker. He was going to ask what Glide meant by 'the obvious', but she had already sprung into the air and disappeared. Before he could ask Scout anything at all, they were loping through the rainforest again.

Light green, dark green, up, down … Deon felt like a kangaroo joey without the benefit of a pouch to hide in.

Scout stopped abruptly. Glide was circling above, and then she descended into the small clearing just ahead of them.

After Scout had freed Deon from the safety belt, Deon sagged to the ground like a wet towel hitting a bathroom floor. He quickly scrambled up onto his shaky legs and followed Scout and Bump as they moved forward.

In the clearing, Glide was ruffling her wings, folding them away. Deon watched as another girl, who had no augz, walked up to Glide and hugged her. A boy who was sitting on the ground behind the girl waved as Scout and Bump approached.

'We have food and new gear,' Glide said, pointing towards Bump.

'I'm so sorry about this mess,' Deon heard the girl say, 'but the Notz threatened us with the blue ring. I didn't want to take the risk that they were bluffing. Once they broke our gear, I wasn't going anywhere, not without Throttle.'

'You did what you had to do, Retro,' said Scout. 'I'm sure we'll catch up to them in time.'

'Good as done—over.'

'Who's that?' the girl called Retro growled when she caught sight of Deon. 'Notz scum!'

'Not Notz—over.'

'Hey, calm down, I'll explain it all to you as you gear up.' Glide took one of the bundles from Bump's pack.

'I'll help Throttle get his gear on,' Scout said.

As Scout approached Throttle, Deon noticed that the other boy didn't look quite right. Throttle wasn't getting up to help put on his own gear.

'This is Deon, and don't get hostile on him, I'll explain soon,' said Scout.

87

'He's not Notz—over,' Bump chirped.

Scout rolled his eyes. 'How'd you get on being without your gear overnight?'

'All good,' Throttle said. 'I love peeing in a cup, lying around listening for wild quollagoes, and wondering if I have what it takes to be a drop-bear whisperer. Or what it would be like to be their next meal.' He smiled. 'Sorry for causing trouble.'

'Hey, it was the Notz that caused this trouble.' Scout straightened Throttle's legs and fitted his frame.

Deon realised that Throttle couldn't move his legs. 'This isn't just augmentation to you, is it?' he said without thinking. 'Oh, sorry.'

'You're right, my unexplained friend.' Throttle flexed his reanimated legs and stood up. 'Without these little beauties I'd be just another gimpy victim of the Notz on the mind mill, and then selected for transplants or brain slavery before I knew it.'

Deon realised he was holding his breath, and trying not to stare. The familiar feeling of not knowing anything crashed over him like a wave.

'Dark but true, as usual, Throttle, but back off a bit,' said Scout. 'Deon's new around here. We want him to help us recover Fuse and Link, so let's not make our guest feel uncomfortable.'

'Nature calls,' said Throttle, and he bounded into the trees.

'He can't walk …' Deon said, running a hand through his hair.

Scout nodded. 'Not without the gear,' he said. 'He's paraplegic, a parkour accident back in the city. If he'd stayed there he probably would've been moved from the hospital to a rehabilitation centre.'

'Is that bad?'

'Rehabilitation means you're in the service of the city, and that's not a good thing. So he let the right people know he was volunteering for augmentation and they sent in a team. Just like that, he was recovered from the hospital and brought to Node for augz.'

'So this Node is around here somewhere and this is where they do the augz, is that right?'

'Well, not in the bower, but yeah. Node's here, and tech is illegal in the cities.'

Deon's head flooded with a tsunami of questions.

End of the Line

'What's the blue ring? Why don't the cities have tech? What's the mind mill? Brain slavery?'

Scout glanced at Deon. 'Slow down, mate, or you're going to blow a connection. Well, you would if you had any.'

'We need to have some food,' said Glide, 'so there's time to answer one question while we eat. And I choose blue ring. At least that one's relevant to our present circumstances.'

Deon frowned. 'Circumstances?'

'Those Notz we're chasing said they're carrying the blue ring,' Glide said, 'so eat and listen. Here's the snack-sized answer. Do you know about blue-ring octopuses?'

'Yeah,' Deon said, 'small octopus, turns blue when it's cranky. If you're stung, paralysis sets in and essentially you're dead. There's no anti-venom, well, in my time there's no anti-venom.'

'There's still no anti-venom now' Glide said. 'The Notz have taken that toxin, created a hybrid bio-cyber virus, and named it the blue ring. Node investigated the claims the Notz had made about having developed what's essentially a weapon, and it's real and dangerous for anyone with augz. If we come into contact the virus, it freezes our gear and we lose our powers.' Glide lifted her arms in a muscle pose and ruffled her wings. 'If the toxin crosses the connection points and enters the bloodstream, we're dead.'

'Tetrodotoxin—over.'

'And you don't have a cure or a firewall against it?'

'No. That's why your uncle was brought here, and how come you accidentally got here.'

'So you knew all along that Nifty was here and you didn't tell me.'

'Well, yeah. Node had a really hard time accepting that you were here, so we had to wait until we got the okay from him before we told you any of this.' Glide shrugged. 'Sorry.'

'But why Nifty?'

'Node holds old records from before the warm. He knew about Nifty's work for the government. Nifty had been involved in the very early stages of developing the virus, so Node arranged to scoop him, hoping he could help develop an antidote.'

Deon nodded. 'And I was brought here by accident. What does—'

Glide held up a hand to stop Deon. 'You've passed your question limit, Deon,' she said. 'When we get Fuse and Link back, they can give you the answers to all your questions.'

'Get them back … just like that?'

'Piece of cake—over.'

Glide circled overhead as Deon felt the straps of the safety harness tighten and heard Scout click the buckle. She pointed up the side of the valley, in the direction that Fuse and Link were being taken. Then she crossed her wrists to indicate that the Notz had tied their hands. Next, she made some signal Deon couldn't decipher.

'Nearly at the top—over,' Bump said.

'Once they've reached the station it won't take long to get the train steamed up,' Scout said to Throttle.

'Yeah,' Throttle agreed. 'Any brainiac taken to the city is on a one-way trip. We need to get there fast.'

The four bouncers made it up the slop at super-human speed. Deon flopped around on Scout's back, trying not to smash his head on the frame and knock himself out.

Throttle stopped for a moment to watch Glide's prompts. 'They're inside the station,' he said, 'but only just. It'll take time to get the train going.'

Spurred on by the urgency, the leaps became even bigger. Deon held on and clenched his muscles, bracing against each jarring rebound. The lushness of the forest valley thinned to scrub as they reached the top of the steep slope.

'End of the line, this train terminates here,' Scout whispered over his shoulder. 'It's not going anywhere.' He released the strap, and Deon puddled onto the ground.

The train station looked to Deon more like an old bomb shelter. It was an oversized concrete building shaped like a Nissan hut. The grey, cracked structure was almost completely covered with vines that had crept up out of the rainforest valley. At the far end of the long half-tube, the double strip of metal train tracks stretched ahead, cutting through the dry scrub. A short distance from the station, there was a circular turning mechanism, and beyond that, the tracks snaked around a curve and disappeared to the west.

Underneath the tangle of vines, Deon could see a peeling sign that actually read *End of the Line*. The scene made him think of bad, black-and-white B-grade movies. *The jig is up. You've reached the end of the line.* He decided to laugh at his joke later, if there was a later.

'Are you sure they're in there?' he asked with a shudder, hoping they could somehow be wrong.

'Fuse got a quick message out to Node before he lost his gear, saying they were with some Notz who planned to take them to the city,' Scout said. 'And this train goes to the city. Besides, Glide saw them go into the station, so, yeah, they're here.'

'At least until the train builds up a head of steam,' said Throttle.

'Steam?' Deon said. 'I thought this was the future, not the past.'

'Like I told you,' said Scout, 'lots of things changed in the chaos after the warm. Instead of taking responsibility for what happened, the Notz blamed technology, so they outlawed most of it and reverted to a bizarre version of the not-so-mighty age of steam.'

'Poo power—over.'

Deon looked at Bump. 'What?'

'The Notz make plenty of human waste in the cities,' Scout explained, 'and they've got to do something with it, so they burn it and make steam to generate power for the city. It fuels the steam engines to make the trains run out here.'

'Why not just use the biogas to run the engines directly?'

'That's a bit too high-tech for the Notz philosophy on technology,' said Throttle.

'Okay, this is how it works,' Scout said. 'The trains burn dried waste, which heats a boiler tank that's filled with wet waste, and as the liquid boils away it makes steam.'

'When the wet waste dries out, it gets shovelled out to become the next batch of poop fuel,' added Throttle. 'Smelly, but it works.'

'But you guys have high-end solar technology.' Deon pointed to their necklaces. 'Why didn't the Notz go that way?'

Scout shrugged. 'Once the rot set in, I guess it was too hard to change people's minds.'

'Change superstitions and lies, you mean,' said Throttle.

'Philosophy time is over, guys,' Glide said from a nearby tree, 'we've got a recovery to do.' She made a clicking sound with her tongue, and her three pets appeared on the branches. 'Fuse and Link had signalled that there were only the two Notz and no others at the station, so I'll send my babies in to put on a cute quollago show and distract the goons. That'll give Deon time to get inside and free them. Okay, Deon?'

'Am I really the only option?' Deon's heart thudded.

'It's like we told you,' Glide said, 'you've got no augz for the sensors to read, so just go in, untie them and get them to the door. These guys will be waiting.'

'Ready—over.'

'You stay with me, Bump,' Glide said, 'for backup.'

'Backup—over.'

Nelly, Rex and Cuddlepie had scuttled through the dry grass to the turntable. They were coming down the tracks towards the train, making a noisy fuss fighting over a piece of fruit.

'We hot enough yet?' came a voice from inside the station.

'Not yet, Norm, but while we're waiting, come and have a look at this.'

When the quollagoes saw the two Notz turn their attention toward them, they rose up onto their hind legs and started a hybrid marsupial-style boxing match on the train tracks. They chittered and squealed as they danced around, slapping each other and grabbing at the fruit as it rolled between them in the middle of the scuffle.

The performance made Deon think of cat videos on the internet. And Glide had been right, the quollago show was distracting. He forced himself to stop watching and turned towards the small side door. He gritted his teeth and twisted the door handle with a sweaty hand. As the door opened, the unmistakable stink of the train's bio-fuel source rammed its way up his nostrils. He stifled a gag and vowed to breathe through his mouth, and only when he absolutely needed to.

His heart was pounding. He stepped through the door and waited for his eyes to adjust to the half-light inside.

Above the sound of his own heartbeat thumping in his ears, and the clicking sound coming from the train as the metal heated and expanded, Deon could hear laughter from the Notz, echoing from the front of the concrete half-tube. He crept across to the back end of the train, blinking through the gloom, searching for Fuse and Link.

The arched hall inside the station looked like an old rail museum. Sheets of dull copper spanned the curve of the roof. In the places where the cracked concrete had leaked, the roof panels were green and bulging with corrosion.

The train was shorter than Deon had expected, just three carriages and an engine up near the front doors of the station. The roof of the carriages had a rounded shape that was similar to the station's roof. This train was very different from the sleek models that Deon used to ride when he lived in the city. It was constructed from panels of dark wood that appeared to be held together with metal straps. The sides of each carriage flared outward so that a wooden skirt covered the wheels. These covers nearly touched the ground, and had hinged access hatches. One was open, and Deon could see the wheel mechanism inside.

The engine was built from metal, and trimmed with carved-wood ornamentation. The train looked more like an old church organ than a transport vehicle. There was a large hopper at the rear of the engine that held the clumps of dried waste. In front of that was a furnace with a boiler on top. The boiler had a small, round copper chimney funnel, which was hissing out wisps of steam. A larger chimney that rose from the furnace was belching out toxic eye-burning poop gas.

Deon put a hand over his mouth, stifling another gag. Squinting into the brightness at the front of the station, he could see the silhouettes of the two Notz, still watching the pet show out on the tracks. Deon moved towards the rear of the train to search for Fuse and Link.

The arched wall at the end of the station housed a huge analogue clock that was set in ornate filigree fretwork. Below the clock was a sign. The words *End of the Line* were painted in flourishing, curled lettering. On each side of the clock were clusters of what looked to Deon like park benches, the polished wooden slats held within dark metal frames.

There was movement in the shadows, on the bench furthest from the door. Fuse and Link sat on the bench, wobbling their heads from side to side. Deon nodded towards them. They lifted their hands slowly and pointed to their feet, indicating the chain that was looped through the metal legs of the bench and shackled to their ankles and wrists.

Deon needed something to cut through those chains. After checking to see if the Notz were still watching the hybrid show, he moved towards the open wheel hatch. There were a few tools lying next to the tracks. He found something that looked like bolt cutters.

He crept through the shadows back to Fuse and Link, and positioned the cutters on the chain around Link's ankles. He clamped down hard, gritting his teeth, hoping he could snap the chain without any noise. He saw the look of recognition on Link's face; he seemed to be struggling not to ask Deon questions. Deon also resisted the urge to pepper Link with the hundreds of questions that were in his own mind.

As soon as Link and Fuse were free, they lowered the pieces of chain to the floor and all three crept towards the door. Deon went through first, and as Link and Fuse pushed through behind him, a storm of sirens started blasting. Fuse slammed the door shut behind him. Deon could see Throttle, Retro and Scout signalling frantically from a distant line of scrub.

A chorus of foul language came from the Notz at the front of the train. They ran inside to check on their captives. There was an ear-splitting whistle from somewhere overhead, followed by growling and then yelling coming from the front of the train.

The quollagoes had moved forward, forming a line of snapping teeth across the tracks. They were growling at the Notz, trapping them inside the station so everyone could get away.

One of the Notz cried out, and there was more swearing. Deon wondered if the quollagoes had been trained to hurt these guys, and how badly. When would Glide call them off?

'Hey, Deon!'

Deon turned. Fuse and Link were already climbing up onto Retro and Scout.

'Hurry up,' Fuse called. 'Get on, we've gotta get out of here.'

Deon bolted for the scrub line, then balked. He realised he would be riding down on Throttle's back, and Throttle was … disabled? No. When Throttle had the augz on, he was stronger than Deon could ever dream of ever being. He clambered up onto Throttle's back, felt the strap tighten as Throttle secured the harness. They all pogoed their way down into the overgrown valley, leaving the Notz and their stinking train behind.

Once they were safe in the cover of the rainforest again, Deon heard a sharp shrill whistle and saw Glide flick across the top of the trees, heading north.

'Mission parameters met—over,' said Bump, as he burst out of the trees and joined the bounding procession.

Deon wondered if the quollogos had backed off. Then he saw the treetops rustle, and Nelly, Rex and Cuddlepie snorted and grunted, springing from tree to tree as they followed Glide. They chittered once, and then disappeared from sight.

Anagram or Dare

The green-green-up-down jostled perambulation back through the rainforest was just as frantic for Deon riding with Throttle as it was with Scout. Deon had seconds only to catch his breath before Throttle started up South Bower. Throttle bounced up along the slanting fin of the buttress root then zigzagged his way up the trunk. The inverted flip onto the platform left Deon breathless.

'Thanks for the ride,' he panted.

'All good,' said Throttle.

The harness fell away, and Deon slid off Throttle's back and stood on shaky legs. He gripped the railing and looked down at the falls, trying to recover. The sun was setting and the shadows were swallowing the lower steps of the falls. A fine mist drifted upwards through the still air, and the water droplets gathered in the treetops, refracting the last of the daylight and causing a swirling cloud of rainbows.

Below, he saw the others arrive. Fuse and Link slipped to the ground, waved to Scout and Bump, and started hiking upstream. Deon's stomach tightened. He had been promised answers to his questions once Fuse and Link were recovered. Now they were off doing whatever and he was being made to wait again.

Deon was hungry for answers to his exponentially growing list of questions about this strange new world. Mostly, he wanted to find out about Nifty. He really wanted to see his uncle, he wanted a huggy dance. Drawing a shuddering breath, he squeezed his hands into determined fists. There were obviously some big-deal things that had to come before Fuse and Link had time to play tour guide for him. He had to be patient and accept that things would happen when they happened; yet another thing in his life he had no control over.

To help shrug off his self-pity, Deon mentally patted himself on the back for the part he had played in the recovery mission. He hadn't felt any confidence when they'd headed out this morning. He hadn't believed he could offer any help to a team that already worked so well together. But as the day had gone on, he'd felt more a part of that team, exchanging information, talking strategy, and not needing to hide that he was smart, the way he'd been doing ever since he'd moved to Moran's Cove. This group had needed him, and he hadn't let them down—or thrown up on anyone.

This recovery stuff is a piece of cake—over. Deon smiled, and watched the colour deepening in the western sky.

'You handled yourself pretty well out there, Deon,' said Throttle, disturbing his thoughts.

'I'm pretty fit,' said Deon, flexing his muscles in a mock boast.

Throttle smiled. 'Good, because I'm sick of piggybacking you, and you need to get across the other side.'

'Yeah,' said Scout, climbing over the railing. 'You need to get across for stink removal before your uncle arrives for our little party.'

'Nifty!' Deon gasped. 'He's really coming?'

'Of course, he's done all he can for now with Node, and we want to thank you both for what you've done for us.'

Throttle handed Scout and Deon a trolley each for the zip-line, climbed over and was gone.

'See you on the other side,' said Scout as he hooked his own trolley, clambered over the railing and pushed off, zinging through the air between the trees.

Suddenly Deon was paying detailed attention to how far below him the creek was, and how thin the cable between the trees now looked. He wiped the sweat from his palms and then wiped the trolley's handgrip on his shirt. The metal was cool in his hands. He hooked it onto the zip-line and then wiped his hands a second time.

He swung a leg over the rail and looked down. The creek was overfull from recent rain and flowing fast. The water looked like a twisting silver ribbon tumbling down the huge stone steps. In each pool, the ribbon of water knotted into a tangled mass of turbulent spray before shooting out and hitting the pool below.

His heartbeat thumped in his ears. *You'd pay big money to do this at a theme park back home.* He told himself to stop worrying and enjoy the ride. He wiped his hands a third time and gripped the trolley.

He leaned out and pushed off. The trolley squealed as it sped along the cable. Deon could smell the hot plastic of the rollers as they warmed up. He twisted so he could see the whole area around the falls, not wanting to waste a second of the ride. He felt moisture on his face from the droplets that were forced up from the cascading water below. Cold air chilled his skin as he flew towards North Bower. He didn't think he would ever get tired of this.

He forgot to brake, hit the landing bag with a clumsy thump and dangled there, smiling like a crazy clown as he bounced several times before finally coming to a stop. When he looked up, Nifty was smiling back at him.

Deon nearly forgot to keep holding on, but Nifty reached out a steadying hand. Deon grabbed it and stepped onto the outside edge of the platform. If it weren't for the feel of Nifty's rough palm against his own, he would have thought it was just a dream. He squeezed Nifty's hand, not wanting to let go.

Nifty placed Deon's hand on the railing. 'Get over here,' he said, holding his arms wide for a hug.

Deon clambered over into the bower, still speechless.

'I want to see this famous huggy dance,' said Glide, breaking the tension of the moment.

'Love to,' said Nifty, closing his arms around Deon.

'Huggy-hug-hug-huuugg,' Nifty sang, as he squeezed Deon in the tightest grip he could ever remember.

Nifty's arms were strong and safe, and Deon felt like he had arrived home after a long, long journey. He made out he was humouring his uncle and the others, but he needed the hug badly. He allowed himself to mould into the tight space inside Nifty's embrace. He breathed in the familiar woolly, slightly metallic, smell of his uncle.

All around him he heard chants of 'huggy-hug-hug-huuugg' and fits of laughter as everyone joined in the dance in a tangle of arms, legs and augz.

When Nifty released Deon, his eyes were glassy with tears. Deon thought his uncle looked old and weary, like he'd gotten to the future the long way round, in centuries instead of moments.

'You look tired,' said Deon, over the noise of the huggy dancers. 'It must've been a long night exchanging information with this … Node.'

'Something like that,' said Nifty. He looked away from Deon.

'What's up?'

'This has all been a lot to take in, boy genius. The whole past-affecting-the future-affecting-the-past thing …' He trailed off and wrapped Deon in another massive hug.

'You found out something that's rattled you, haven't you?'

'Yeah, I did, even though technically it hasn't really happened yet.'

'Is Mum all right?' Deon's face flooded with heat.

'Your mum is fine, was fine and will be fine. Ehh, time travel, it's left me feeling a little tense about my tenses.' He laughed unconvincingly.

'But I've been gone for more than a day,' Deon said. 'She'll be frantic.'

'Don't worry about your mum. Apparently, when we get back it'll be the same time as when we left. Node says the scoop is like a slingshot. It grabs you and pulls you out of your own time and into this one, but when it releases you, you get flung back to where and when you started.'

'I want to know how that can work, but logic's telling me the question is too hard to get an answer to.'

'Your assumption is correct,' said Nifty. 'I can't work it out either—well, not yet.'

'But can you at least tell me why we're here?'

'Why *you're* here is easy. The first time was an accident, and the second time was an accident.'

Deon groaned. 'Time travel hasn't changed your skill at comedy.'

'Thank you.' Nifty bowed.

Deon shook his head and smiled. 'So what caused this accident?'

'Mistaken identity,' said Nifty. 'They use DNA to locate someone for the scoop, and the first time, at the pole, they mistook you for me.'

'And *you're* here because …'

'I'm here because, well, it seems that information about my secret work for the military survived in Node's records and he—um, it—tracked me down.'

'But you'd shown us some of your inventions once they were declassified, and they were all hardware. They said this was a virus.'

'The really secret part of my work, before I retired, was designing pretty nasty computer viruses, and also some hefty firewalls and guard bots. The military was changing the way they did their war thing.' Nifty shuddered. 'The real battles were starting to be fought online, and I was a soldier.'

'So you're helping with the blue-ring problem, whatever that is.'

'Blue ring, shmoo-ring, it's time to throw a fawn on the barbie—over.'

'That's prawn, not fawn, Bump,' Glide said. 'And prawns are extinct, so let's put some chicken burgers on the barbie instead.' Glide had already lost her augz and her stink, and was issuing orders from the kitchen. 'No one eats if they stink,' she announced over her shoulder.

The others took the hint and headed upstairs, but Deon lingered close to Nifty before following reluctantly.

Those chicken burgers smell amazing,' Deon said, as he stepped onto the curved platform.

'Kinda chicken—over,' said Bump.

'Kinda chicken?'

'*Aves T. Moluccas*—over.'

Deon raised a questioning eyebrow.

'It's not just prawns that went extinct, but poultry is poultry,' Fuse said, carrying a plate of round patties, 'and these kinda-chicken burgers are extremely tasty.'

Scout was flipping the kinda-chicken burgers that were sizzling and splattering on the hot grill, and Nifty went to help. Before long Deon was focused only on his stomach, and the few hundred remaining questions faded while he hurried to help in the kitchen to speed up preparation and shorten the wait time until dinner.

'Well, *Aves T. moluccus* burgers are delicious,' Deon said around a mouthful of burger. 'Can you tell me now that I'm nearly finished what species of burger this is?'

'It's a larger native wading bird,' said Fuse. 'Node said they used to be a bit of a pest way back, and since the flooding they really took over so there are plenty to go around.'

'They're chicken sized, free range, and a good source of protein,' said Scout.

'Dumb and easy to catch,' added Retro.

'Dump chooks!' spluttered Deon, horrified. Everyone around the table shrugged, not understanding, and kept munching.

'Too funny.' Nifty kept chewing, shaking his head and grinning. 'White ibis.'

'Ibis burgers—over,' Bump said, with his mouth full.

Deon swallowed hard on his last, half-chewed mouthful. He had a big swallow of water to try and get the taste out of his mouth. Then he quickly reached for some fruit.

'Have you figured out how far in the future we are?' Deon asked Nifty, biting into the fruit and trying not to think about the dump chook he had just scoffed down.

'I've got a count of days since he—Node was brought online, so I could do the maths, but I still wouldn't know what the exact date is.'

'Rough estimate?'

'A couple of centuries, at least,' said Nifty.

'I'm trying to understand all this, but it doesn't make sense,' Deon said. 'These guys—the Havz—and this Node, all seem so totally *Star Trek*. But the Notz seem to be rubbing two sticks together. The Notz are scared of technology, but they've developed a virus that can attack computerised technology and human organisms simultaneously. It doesn't make sense that those cowboys can be such a threat.'

'Well, that's sort of my fault, and Node's.'

'How?'

'The blue-ring was developed from something I'd started long ago. Node was searching through lost files of my top-secret stuff and found it. It ended up stored in his temporary files, which weren't password protected, so before Node could secure all the files, the Notz got hold of it.'

'How could they do that if they don't have the internet, plexus, whatever?'

'Yeah, they do,' Fuse interrupted. 'The plexus is organic, mostly.' He tapped the side of his head. 'It's us, the brainiacs. We can connect to Node and access any info he allows.'

'So the Notz have the plexus, too?'

'They have a simpler version,' said Link. 'That's what they use all the gimps and crazies for, they wipe them and wire them up.'

'All the who?'

'Their words, not ours,' Scout continued. 'They take advantage of people that are disabled, weak or alone and can't protect themselves, and use them to connect to the plexus.'

'And that's how they got the blue-ring?'

'Sort of,' said Fuse. 'But the connection is … less effective. If they want a firm connection with Node they need one of us.'

'They tried to kidnap you today,' Deon said. 'So that's happened before? To someone else?'

'Yeah, two years ago they got my brother Hal,' said Glide quietly.

'And?'

'And, using him, they got the info they needed to develop the blue-ring,' Glide said, putting all her attention into collecting plates from the table.

'And now,' Throttle said, 'it's time to play Anagram or Dare.' The mood lightened with the change of subject.

Glide looked relieved that the attention had shifted from her. 'I'll get the chocolate.'

'I'll get the tiles and the dare barrel,' said Throttle.

'There's still chocolate in the future, very cool,' said Deon.

'Very rare—over.'

'It's almost impossible to get,' Glide said, giving Deon a stare that said no more questions or else. She took the stack of plates and escaped into the kitchen. He took the hint and kept quiet.

'Chocolate is like sweet gold,' said Retro, 'so we only use it to reward the anagram master.'

'For the newcomers to Anagram or Dare, here are the rules,' said Throttle, sounding like a game-show host. 'We divide the letter tiles evenly among the players. The person whose birthday is soonest plays first then it's clockwise around the group. Lay out a word, add to an existing word, or use a letter to make a crossed word.'

'Like Scrabble,' said Deon.

'If you say so.' Throttle continued. 'First player with no tiles is the anagram master for that round and gets a choc. The last player with tiles chooses a dare card from the barrel and entertains us with an ill-conceived acrobatic feat. No augz allowed, especially you guys.' He pointed to Link and Fuse and tapped the side of his head.

'Node will dob—over.'

Deon looked at Throttle, who still had his leg frames on.

Throttle noticed and patted the frames. 'These are just my pyjama legs, no super power here.'

Glide was the first to place all her tiles, and she made a loud, slurping display of eating her chocolate prize.

Deon was the fourth to finish behind Nifty, and then Bump, who was better than Deon thought he would be at playing with words. In the end it came down to just Link and Retro.

'Yes! And even though one of her two remaining letters is a zed,' Retro boasted, 'she makes this one into ozone and saves her augmented butt from the peril barrel.' She bowed and blew some kisses.

'Now for the real entertainment,' said Throttle, grabbing the small red barrel.

Link groaned and put his hand into the barrel as though it was full of funnel-web spiders. He drew out a small card and handed it to Throttle.

'Ladies, gentlemen and Havz of all ages, for your entertainment our daredevil comrade will … ride the wild helix.'

Link groaned even louder. Then he trudged to the top of the spiral staircase that coiled around the tree trunk and sat on the bannister rail.

'Remember, legs on the outside of the rail,' reminded Scout, smiling broadly.

Link swung his legs over and held on.

'And no hands,' added Retro.

'Centrifugal force can be a real downer,' said Fuse.

'Newton's rules rule—over,' said Bump.

'Where's the first-aid kit?' mumbled Nifty.

'Go.' Link let go and started sliding. He built up speed exponentially. He pulled thoughtful faces as he tilted his weight, trying to compensate for the centrifugal force. This

111

worked well for three-quarters of his trip to the bottom, but then he overbalanced and flew through the air, landing on Retro.

Cheers and laughter erupted. Deon noticed that Retro and Link spent a little longer tangled up with each other than they really had to. The first-aid kit was not required, and Glide decided that the stunt was so entertaining Retro and Link deserved a chocolate each.

They played three more rounds, with the chocolate going to Retro, then Deon and then Throttle. Bump, Scout and Glide all gave spectacular shows when they lost and had to draw from the dare barrel. As the moon rose above the trees, the game fizzled out and they dimmed the lights.

Deon settled back with a cup of the mysterious Milo-type drink to watch the night sky. 'Why do you think it's all happened in this area?' he asked Nifty.

'Why what's happened?'

'This camp and Node,' Deon said. 'What makes this place the centre for weird science and time travel?'

All the other chatter ceased as everyone listened to Nifty's answer.

'There are caves here, in the cliffs. I never saw them, ever, even with all the exploring your dad and I did here when we were kids, or when I hiked up here when I moved to town. Node isn't mobile and needs to be cool and secure, so it makes sense to hide in the caves.'

'Massive coincidence.' Deon shook his head. 'When do I get to see Node?'

'Node's pretty busy working on the blue ring and overseeing things.'

'Hey, how did Node know where you were? That scoop thing was pretty specific. The first time, Node knew exactly where you and I usually go running, and that's how I got my accidental taste of time travel. And then the second time, Node just happened to know exactly where your shed was, and I had the best, or worst, timing and did a bit more time travel.'

'Very timely, boy genius.'

'Not an answer,' said Deon. 'How did Node know how to find you? Yesterday, Glide and Scout said that most of the information had been scrambled in something called the chaos.'

'I'm working on an answer to that one.'

'No, you're sitting on the answer to that one.' Deon stared at Nifty. 'That's your top-secret face, so what are you not telling me?'

'Not yet, boy genius.' This time even the others looked puzzled about what Nifty was withholding.

'Glide, I was wondering something.' Nifty turned in his seat and changed the subject. 'You said that prawns were extinct, but I used to catch fish at these falls a couple of centuries ago. Are there still fish in the pools?'

'Catch 'em and kiss 'em—over.'

'There are fish,' said Glide, 'but mainly in the deep pool at the base of the falls. Why?'

'Deon and I were planning to go out fishing before all this happened, so why don't we do a spot of fishing tomorrow?

I promised Node that I'd hang around and we'd work on the blue-ring for a couple of days, so why not use the time relaxing?'

'Nicely orchestrated diversion, Uncle Nifty,' Deon said with a smile.

Nifty grinned. 'I do what I can, boy genius. Now let's get some sleep, we're going fishing in the morning.'

Gone Fishing

The morning was still. The falls had returned to their pre-storm calm, and the valley was quiet. The zing of the trolley on the zip-line echoed in the space between the trees. Deon could easily have used the rappel chair to get down from North Bower, but he chose another ride across to South Bower on the zip-line—just because he could.

The air was an icy smack in the face as he flew along the line. His eyes watered and lines of tears trailed back across his temples.

Glide had retold boastful stories as she offered tips for fishing over breakfast. She assured Nifty that the extra water that had run over the falls in the last few days would have washed lots of fish down into the bottom pool.

'Fish for dinner—over,' Bump had called as Deon climbed over the railing to follow Nifty back to South Bower on the zip-line.

Shafts of sunlight pierced the canopy, causing bright-dark-bright strobes as Deon flew along the cable. He was full of smiles as he hit the landing platform, stowed his trolley, and flipped himself into the rappel chair. He flicked off the chair's brake and sped down the vertical cable—with his stomach following a few seconds later.

Nifty was waiting for him when he unharnessed at the buttressed base of South Bower. 'Fun?' he asked, smiling up at Deon. He was crouched next to the first pool in the cascade, watching the falling water churn as it hit the still surface of the pool. Deon sat down and dangled his legs over the drop-off.

'Massive fun, I don't think riding that flying fox will ever get old.'

'I concur.' Nifty stood up and slung the backpack over his shoulder. 'They don't catch fish with rods, but Glide gave me some nets, so netting will have to do.'

'Are you sure we should go?' Deon thought he'd try once more to get Nifty to open up about his top-secret Node stuff. 'Maybe we should go and check with Node to see if we can help with the blue-ring problem.'

'We don't need to do anything except go fishing. I made a promise to you, and I'm about two and a half centuries late in keeping that promise, so we're going fishing.' He slapped Deon on the back and steered him to the first of the giant steps. 'Anyway, Node said the work would take twenty-four hours, and that's hours away.'

Deon puffed out an over-loud sigh. There was a rustling sound overhead, which he assumed was Nelly, Rex and Cuddlepie playing in the treetops. Turning, he lowered himself towards the footholds and climbed down the rock face to the next level.

Nifty followed him. He was mumble-hum-singing one of his nineties playlist songs. 'I don't ever hmm-hmm-hmmm, hmm-hmm-hmm-hmm.'

Nifty replayed his playlist constantly, so Deon had heard them all. He had to admit that the tunes were catchy, contagious even. He tried not to sing along, knowing Nifty was attempting to fill his head with songs so he wouldn't ask any questions. Deon decided to let Nifty have his way for now. Being in Nifty's musical vibe was nice; he could wait a while to ask his questions.

By the time they'd climbed down the rock steps to the base of the cascade, Deon was singing along. Then Nifty got stuck, looping one phrase: 'Hmmm-hmm-hmmm-hmmm-hmmm, like to say, hmm-hmmm-hmm don't know hmmm.'

'You've looped on those words five times, Nifty.' Deon stared at his uncle. 'So what are the things you need to tell me?' he said, locking Nifty's gaze.

For a second, Nifty looked like a roo caught in the headlights of a truck. Then his face smoothed and became a cheesy grim. 'How about this? The wheels on the bus, hmm-hmm-hmm-hm-hm …'

'Groan,' said Deon.

Nifty shrugged off his backpack and dropped it on the ground next to the pool. 'Okay, you ready to catch some fish?' He unzipped the bag and started pulling out gear. 'Glide said the fish aren't used to people, so if we get into the water and

117

stand still until they forget about us, they should swim right into the nets.'

'How convenient. I guess Bump will get his fish dinner tonight instead of dump-chook.' In spite of Deon's frustrations about Nifty's top-secret mood, he laughed.

'It'll be a fish feast. Come and grab a net.'

They both stripped down to their undies and slid into the pool. The water was icy, but refreshing after they'd become so hot from climbing down the steps. The trees around the pool were a towering wall of green and shadows. In the shelter of the lower forest, the air was still. Everything was quiet except for the stream of water flowing over the rock ledge above and hitting the pool with a fizz.

They left the nets on the rocks and swam into the bubbling undercurrent at the base of the fall. Directly under the flow, it felt like being in a washing machine; the water tried to tumble them like they were old socks.

Pulling free of the dumping water, they glided over to the other side of the pool where the water was calm, and floated in a patch of sunlight. The sun bounced off the water, making random patterns of blinding light that reflected at odd angles and speckled the trees around the pool with points of light. Where the water was in shadow, Deon could see beneath the surface. Silver flashes twisted as a few large fish swam around, investigating the new objects in their pond.

Nifty drifted back across the pool and picked up the nets. He decided on a position he thought would be the best for catching fish and gestured for Deon to join him.

'I know this trip is meant to distract me from asking the hundreds of questions I have to ask, but it's not working.' Deon said, after joining Nifty and taking a net.

'Fine, I'll see if I can answer a couple of questions while we stand still and wait for the fish to forget we're here.'

'You will?' Deon fumbled with the net. 'Okay, I noticed that the others say "he" instead of "it" when they talk about Node, and you sometimes do, too. What's that about?'

After a long pause, Nifty's top-secret face melted into an answer. 'I think it's because Node connects with the world through the brainiacs, so when he—it—talks through them, it seems more like a person.'

Nifty's answer felt a bit made up, but Deon decided it was better not to complain and just keep his uncle talking. 'So the brainiacs let Node take them over?'

'Yeah, but they only do it for short periods of time and it's voluntary. That's how they get the augz done. Node uses their hands to do the work.'

'Creepy. Wouldn't the connection to Node make the brainiacs sound robotic when they talk? Even though it's talking through a person, it should still sound like a machine, shouldn't it?'

A flash of *top secret* ran across Nifty's face. 'I can't really tell you much more than that, Deon.'

'You can't, or you won't?'

'I got one! Look, it just swam straight into the net.'

'Convenient timing,' huffed Deon.

Nifty lifted the net and waded over to transfer the fish to the holding net he had anchored to a rock at the edge of the

119

pool. Then he came back and settled in to wait for the next fish. 'Next question,' he said.

'Link said something about what the Notz do if they catch a brainiac. He said they "wipe them". What does that mean?'

'That one I don't know, Deon. Maybe they do something with the data the brainiacs hold, like deleting files or stealing them.' Nifty jerked his net up again. 'This one is huge,' he said, and waded across to put the second fish with the other captive.

'Do you think it would hurt to get the augz implanted?' Deon asked when he returned.

'I'd hope there would be some sort of anaesthetic or pain blocker for the process. Why, are you planning to get some fitted? I think your mum would kill me really quickly if you went home looking all robot-y.'

'No, but how amazing would it be to be able to access all the info from the net—plexus, whatever—directly into your brain.'

Nifty's smile faded. He looked out into the trees.

'What?'

Nifty shrugged and the look was gone. 'You've got one!' He lifted Deon's arm in the air like he was a champion. 'You're shivering. Come on, I think three fish is enough for now. Let's warm up in the sun and have something to eat.'

They climbed out of the pool and stretched out on a warm, smooth rock to dry. They ate something Scout had called 'trail bars' when he'd handed them over that morning.

'I thought I'd lost you, too,' Deon said quietly, keeping his eyes on the tops of the trees. 'When you disappeared that night.' He took a deep breath. 'It was like when Dad was gone. That's why I had to go after you.'

'I'm sorry I scared you.'

'It wasn't your fault. It looks like Node had you pegged as the guy that could fix all its problems, just like you do for me.' Deon nudged his uncle with his elbow. Nifty nudged back.

After a few moments, Deon said, 'Hey, Nifty, yesterday you said the past affects the future and that affects the past. Did you say that because you started making the virus back in the past, and now it's affecting the future? And that's why they need your help now, to fix the problem?'

'Something like that.' Nifty sat up and gave Deon his changing-the-subject smile. 'There's a thing in sci-fi called "the bootstrap paradox". The theory is that if you could go back in time you could help an event or a person—you know, give them knowledge or a skill—and that would make an event happen in the future that might not have happened otherwise.'

Deon nodded. 'Then the person from the future would affect the past. And the person or thing in the past would change the future, if everything turned out right.'

'That's right, but sometimes it can happen by accident.'

'Like me being here when it should only be you.'

'Something like that.'

'Nifty, you're getting vague again.'

'I know, and I'm not keeping secrets, not really. I'm just delivering the info in snack-sized chunks.'

'No. You're withholding information.'

'Okay, boy genius, from here on, no secret-squirrel stuff.'

121

Deon smiled and formed his next question. 'Have you figured out how Node knew exactly where and when to find you?'

Nifty drew in a long breath and sighed. 'Node always knew where we were—'

'What's up, Nifty?' Deon sat up quickly. His uncle's face had gone slack and his eyes were glassy, empty. Deon turned to see what had caused Nifty to stop mid-sentence.

Nifty suddenly went limp and sagged onto the rock, making a thud as his head landed. Deon reached over to check his uncle's breathing. It was shallow and slow. Deon felt a sharp sting as something hit his shoulder and then, in a noisy rush, the shiny pool and the green wall of trees faded to black.

Cuddlepie

Hot puffs of fruity, meaty funk were blowing against Deon's face as he came to. The puffs were accompanied by soft, chittering growls. As the blackness receded, he felt a heavy weight on his chest. The growling puffs grew louder. The thing pressing on his chest was shifting, shuffling, as he tried to move and regain ownership of his limp body.

The chittering grew louder still, and Deon could feel the spike of claws on his bare skin. His brain's first lucid thought was: *Drop-bear!*

The huffing was now coming in rapid gusts, and then there was a blood-curdling yowl, which was answered by another yowl from somewhere in the forest above him. Then there was a piercing whistle.

Deon forced himself to open his eyes. 'Cuddlepie?'

Big, dark eyes stared down at him across a furry, pointed nose. The quollago sat on his chest, making a sound that was half giggle, half cough, and then she sat up on her hind legs and yowled again. Deon heard a distant but familiar crashing sound, and then heard Glide's voice.

'Cuddlepie!' she called from somewhere above him in the trees.

Cuddlepie made a happy squealing noise. Nelly dropped from the branches and landed silently on the grass beside Deon and grunted. He jumped with the shock, and this made Cuddlepie spring from his chest and chitter her complaints. The wall of green trembled as Scout burst through, carrying a glazed-looking Link on his back.

'Where's Nifty?' Scout asked urgently.

'What?' Deon was suddenly fully awake. The rock next to him was bare. His heart pounded up into his throat. Heat raced across his skin. 'Nifty passed out, right here. Where is he?' He couldn't breathe. Twisting to look around the clearing, he saw everything as a tilting, green blur.

Scout crouched next to him, reaching out a steadying hand. 'You were knocked out, too.'

'I felt a sting on my shoulder. Then everything went black. Then Cuddlepie was here. Where's Nifty?' he said again.

Glide circled down out of the trees and kneeled beside Deon, leaving her wings open and ruffled. 'You okay? What's this?' she said, picking up a leaf and wrapping it around something that was piercing the skin on Deon's shoulder. 'Looks like some kind of bur.'

Bump, who had stumbled out of the undergrowth behind her, said, 'Cat's head—over.'

'I bet it's covered with whatever they used to knock you and Nifty out,' Glide said.

'I didn't hear any shot,' said Deon.

'It would've been something low tech. A slingshot, some kind of bow or small catapult,' said Glide.

Link refocused. 'Rex is following them, Node's picking up his tracker signal. They're heading to the end of the line, but they're moving too fast, which means they're not on foot.'

'It sounds like those goons we shamed when we recovered Link and Fuse have got some kind of backup. If so, they might not take as long to get the train steamed up,' said Glide. 'We better hurry.'

'I'll let Fuse know so he and Throttle can get things ready.' Link zoned out again as he sent the message.

'Good to go—over.' Bump said, helping Deon struggle into his clothes. Then he picked him up and bounded up the first rock step, and zigzagged up the falls. Deon's head spun with each bounce. When they reached South Bower, everything was a rush of chaotic preparations.

'Who's being Node's hands today?' asked Glide.

'Me,' said Fuse.

'I'll take Fuse and head up to the cave,' Throttle said. 'I'm sure Node will need the extra help now.'

'I'll take Link—over,' said Bump.

'Scout, Retro, let's go,' said Glide.

'I'm going, too,' said Deon.

'I don't think so,' said Glide sternly. 'You don't have a role to play in this recovery.'

125

'My role is that he's my uncle.' Deon glared at Glide, struggling to hide his threatened tears.

Glide hesitated. 'Scout, will taking Deon slow you down?'

'No.'

'Okay, you're with Scout, Deon. Retro, save your strength for the return trip with Nifty.'

'And the fight.' Retro smiled.

'And the fight,' Glide agreed. 'So, are we all good, people?'

'All good,' they chorused.

'Node says they're already climbing up to the station,' said Link.

Deon heard the buckle click, and in seconds he was plunged back into the green-green-up-down madness of traversing the rainforest. The speed at which they moved made yesterday's recovery mission seem like a walk in the park. There was no leapfrogging today, just a silent push forward. With the poison still in his system, combined with the relentless pace and the blurring world of green, he lost the argument with his stomach and threw up. The spray of vomit chunks flew back behind him as Scout sped towards the end of the line.

This Train Terminates

The green-green-up-down blur finally slowed, then stopped. Scout turned back and forth, looking around the area, and with each turn Deon felt his brain rattle, but he saw they were on familiar ground. They had reached the end of the valley near the station. Tracks led a few metres up the slope, stopping at a small four-wheeled vehicle with a rack at the rear. They bounded up for a closer look.

'Electric,' Scout said. He pointed to lines of crushed ferns. 'Those are older tracks leading down the slope.'

'So that's why they could move so fast,' said Deon. 'Even with Nifty unconscious.'

'It must be out of charge,' said Scout. 'At least that's slowed them down a bit.'

Above them on the plateau, they could just see the concrete curve of the station roof. Beyond it, a column of smoke was rising into the air. There was a sudden belch of steam.

'Train's already hot—over.' Bump shook his head.

'We're out of time,' said Scout.

Glide swooped down from the station and signalled for them to hurry. The others sprang off up the slope ahead of them.

'I'll go around wide,' said Retro. 'Then I'll hide at the tree line in front of the station.' She disappeared into the trees.

Deon and Scout moved up the slope towards the station. At the rear of the huge building, Scout barely had time to release Deon from the harness before the train spewed out a huge plume of steam. There was a grinding crunch as the drive rods pushed power from the engine. The wheels skidded into motion on the steel tracks and the train lurched forward out of the concrete half-tunnel of the station.

'Let's catch ourselves a train,' said Scout. 'If we get inside the station, we can run up behind it where they can't see us.'

'Might hear us—over.' Bump looked up at the roof and smiled. He sprang upward and came crashing down on the rusted siren that was connected to the door sensor. It crumpled under his weight and spat a shower of sparks as he tugged it free of its wires. Then he kicked it into the scrub. 'All aboard—over.' Bump jumped off the roof and landed back next to Link. 'Upsy-daisy—over.'

Link jumped onto Bump's back. Deon scrambled back up onto Scout and hung on tightly as they all jammed through the narrow door at the rear of the station. They ran along the tracks, chasing the train as it started pulling away.

'Thanks, Bump,' Scout called out. 'At least they won't hear us coming, and if they see us—'

'The fight starts sooner—over.'

As the train passed the turntable, Retro leapt from the trees on the right side of the train, arched high into the air, somersaulted and landed lightly on the roof of the third and last car. She climbed down from the roof on a flimsy ladder, opened the door at the rear of the carriage and swung inside. Holding the door wide open, she stood ready to help the uninvited passengers get on board.

Scout sprang up, landed badly, and his toes slipped off the edge of the doorway. As he grabbed the ladder, Deon's stomach lurched and he tightened his grip. Retro reached out, grabbed Deon by the shirt and pulled him and Scout inside. Scout sprang to his feet, dumping Deon onto the floor, and helped grab Bump as he and Link crashed in behind them.

'Welcome aboard,' said Retro.

'Now all we need to do is stop the Notz, stop the train and get Nifty back.' said Scout. 'Easy.'

Link's eyes glazed over for a moment 'You have one hour before the train reaches the next station,' Node said, through Link. 'Then there'll be more Notz to deal with.'

Deon noted that although the voice was Link's, the phrasing wasn't. This must somehow be Node speaking directly, but the speech didn't sound automated in the way that Deon had expected.

'This train terminates—over.'

'It sure will,' said Retro. 'What weapons does Node say they have, Link?'

Link glazed. 'They have tools on the train that could be repurposed. They have the bow or slingshot they used to launch the burs. We have to assume they do have the blue-ring.'

'I wonder what their range is for shooting those burs,' Retro said.

'Let's hope they think their electric buggy will give them enough of a head start that they don't need many weapons,' said Deon.

'If they have the blue-ring on any of those burs then they *don't* need many weapons,' Node said through Link.

'Lucky us—over.'

Scout stared past the rows of leather passenger seats towards the connecting door at the front of the carriage. 'Since no one's here yet, we can assume they haven't noticed our arrival.'

'It makes sense that they'd all stay together,' Retro said. 'They might all be in the first carriage.'

'Yeah, they wouldn't all fit in the engine cab,' added Link, in his usual tone.

Scout leaned out and grabbed the ladder outside the door at the rear of the carriage. 'I'm going up on the roof for a minute to see if Glide's seen anything.' He climbed up and in moments was on the roof.

Deon saw Glide weaving in and out of the tree line, trying to stay out of sight. Scout must have got her attention, because she started signalling: *two in the engine, three in the first carriage*. She added a quick pat on her heart.

Scout clambered back through the carriage door. 'Five including Nifty,' he said. 'Two Notz on the engine and two more in the first carriage with Nifty.'

Nifty was only two carriages away. Deon trembled. He had to do something.

'So we just sneak up on the first two and take them out,' said Retro. 'Then—'

'Sorry to be critical of your plan at this point,' Deon interrupted, 'but although you guys have lots of skills, even superpowers, sneaking isn't one of them.'

Scout smiled. 'It's a consequence of the hardware.'

'How about Link and I do the sneaking and you guys act as backup?' Deon suggested.

Link smiled and nodded his agreement.

'I'll go out again and walk up front on the roof,' said Scout. 'From there I'll be able to watch out for anyone coming from the engine.'

'I guess we'll just have to wait until you need our superpowers,' Retro said to Deon.

'Sounds like a plan—over.'

Sneaking

A foul-smelling wind swept over Deon and Link as they crossed the flimsy iron coupling bridge that connected the third and second carriages. The fumes from the smokestack stung Deon's eyes. His heart was thumping faster than the frantic *click-thump* of the racing wheels below them. He turned the grimy metal handle and eased open the door to the second carriage.

This carriage was identical to the one they had just left; they both looked like passenger cars on a train in an old western movie. The air inside was hot and full of the acrid, buttery smell of polished leather. There was a narrow walkway between the high-backed, copper-studded seats. Each empty seat had its own copper-framed window. Perfect for shooting baddies out of, he thought. The polished wooden floor and fancy lace curtains reminded Deon of his grandmother's house.

The train rocked and juddered as it lurched around an unexpected bend in the line. Deon made a startled noise and they both groped for a handhold on the seats. Link missed and fell onto the wooden floor. Deon squeezed behind one of the seats and pulled Link with him. The noise of the train should have masked the sound, but they still froze, waiting to see if they'd been heard.

Seconds ticked by. Deon wiped the stinging residue from his watering eyes, and took a deep breath to clear his lungs and try to calm his pounding heart. Nifty was just metres away, he told himself. It would all be over soon, and the last recovery had been easy. But his heart would not be calm.

No one came in from the first carriage; they had not been discovered. They stood and walked confidently to the front of the carriage. The door burst open. They dropped to the floor and tried to scramble behind the seats. Deon recognised Scout's boots and nudged Link.

'See, I can sneak,' Scout whispered from the doorway, a massive grin on his face.

'Not funny,' Link hissed, holding his hand over his heart.

'What are you doing here, Scout?' Deon asked.

'Planning a diversion,' he said. 'I'll go back up on the roof, sneak to the front of the first carriage and make some noise to get the Notz' attention. They'll come out on the coupling bridge, and when they're close enough for me to … all the rest is just messy details. As soon as the Notz are outside, you two can …' Scout paused, raised an eyebrow. 'Feel free to share your plan now, guys.'

'Your diversion idea sounds great,' said Deon, struggling to think of ideas. Then he saw a cabinet on the wall, opened it, and pulled out a large wrench that looked like it could be used to connect the coupling bridge. 'You could smack the Notz with this,' he said to Link, handing over the wrench. He hoped Link would have the guts to use it because he doubted he had the nerve to do it himself.

No, he thought, I could do it for Nifty. He took another heavy spanner-like tool from the cabinet for himself.

Scout scrambled across to the rear of the first carriage and up the ladder before disappearing onto the carriage roof. Deon and Link moved out onto the rattling coupling bridge and waited for signs of Scout's diversion. Link pressed his face against the window in the door, positioning his eye to see through the gap in the lace curtain. Deon stood on the tiny trembling platform behind him, trying not to breathe in the noxious stink billowing around them.

Finally Link elbowed Deon hard in the ribs. 'Now!'

Link opened the door slightly. They could hear voices at the front of the carriage talking in urgent tones. Deon and Link slipped inside the carriage and squeezed in behind the last seat. Deon pushed the door closed, holding his breath to see if the Notz had heard the click of the door latch, but they were deep in conversation.

'It was probably just a bird,' said one of the Notz.

'But it cracked the window, Bob,' said the other.

'Bet it's got a headache now,' said the one called Bob.

'Yeah, just like our special passenger here.' He turned towards Nifty. 'Bet you've got a headache, too, mate.'

'He'll have one when the mind mill finishes its job,' said Bob.

Link went pale. 'Mind mill,' he muttered, shaking his head. 'What?'

'Bad. We need to hurry,' Link whispered.

No one had gotten around to answering Deon's questions about the mind mill yet, but Link looked terrified. Adrenaline flooded through Deon. He wanted to run at Bob and his buddy, smash both men with the weird heavy tool, and get Nifty away from danger. He started to move out of their hiding spot, but Link grabbed him and held him down. Deon resisted. Link shook his head and his eyes were pleading.

Deon's vision blurred with tears. He struggled to take a breath as his heart thumped between his lungs.

'Soon … soon,' Link whispered. He released Deon's arms and wriggled past him to look at what was happening. Then he nodded and gestured for Deon to chance taking a look.

Peering up over the seat, Deon could see that this carriage was finished differently to the others. Pairs of seats faced each other, and in between each pair was a small table. The two Notz had closed the front door and returned to their seat at the first table with their backs to Link and Deon. Nifty was sitting on the other side of the table. He was strapped to the seat by two broad belts crossing his chest. He was wearing something that looked like a cross between a leather swimming cap and a bicycle helmet.

Deon chanced a signal to let Nifty know that help was on the way. Nifty gave no reaction.

Something loud thumped against the window again.

'Stupid birds,' said Bob.

There was no reaction from Nifty, not even a blink.

Link nudged Deon and pointed to a pile of Notz equipment on the seat opposite them. He reached across and lifted something off the seat. It was narrow, long and made of wood, and it had metal attachments. There was a loop of metal halfway along the underside. If the object were a gun, the loop would be the trigger. On the upper side, a cat's head bur was held in a narrow channel that ran the length of the wooden shaft.

Deon thought it looked like some kind of launching device—a slingshot-gun hybrid. Two loops at one end held a thick strap that was stretched and held in place with a hook and spring that connected to the 'trigger' on the underside.

Link inspected the device then blanked out for a moment. When his focus returned, he nodded confidently. He placed the heavy wrench on the floor, and began checking and handling the weapon as though he'd used one many times before.

'This bur is the ammunition, and it's probably covered in the drug that was used on you and Nifty,' Link whispered. 'At least, I hope it's just a knockout drug and not blue-ring. The blue-ring doesn't work on the Notz, and that would ruin our plans.'

'If you aim for the one on the left, I'll get the other one on the right.' Deon lifted his spanner-weapon; he couldn't wait to avenge his uncle.

'Stay down and get ready.' Link stood and aimed.

The bur hit Bob's unnamed friend in the back of his bald scalp and he crumpled to the wooden floor in the aisle between the seats. Bob turned, took one look at Link and the now unloaded weapon in his hands, leapt over the seat and bolted down the carriage toward him.

Link opened the carriage door and reversed outside quickly, slamming the door in front of Bob. Deon remained wedged behind the seat. His hands were sweaty as he tightened his grip on the heavy spanner.

In five hurried, angry steps, Bob had reached the last table nook. He reached out a hand to pull the door open.

Deon hesitated, a high-speed stream of thoughts ploughing through his brain. *I'm about to slam someone in the head. That's not what I do. That's what Johno does.* His stored anger flared inside him. *Johno and the zombies hurt me. The Notz have hurt Nifty.* In a split second, he aimed, then closed his eyes and swung the spanner upwards with as much force as he could.

The sound Bob made told Deon that he'd hit him in the guts or maybe the chest. Not good enough. He opened his eyes and saw that Bob had come to a sudden stop. He was buckled over, making grunting-gulping sounds. His eyes were level with where Deon was crouched behind the seat.

Bob let go of his stomach and reached to grab Deon. Deon scuttled backwards, but Bob's meaty hand grabbed his shirt. The train lurched around a corner. Bob over-balanced, toppled forward and slammed his head into the thick, steel carriage door. He lay very still on his huge gut. His face was slack and scrunched sideways. A trail of drool was running from his gaping mouth and pooling on the polished wooden floor.

Deon scrambled over the seat to make sure he was clear in case the man regained consciousness, but Bob remained deathly still, his head wedged up against the door. Deon reached out a foot and kicked Bob's leg to see if he was really unconscious. No reaction.

Link pushed back into the carriage, slamming the door into Bob's head and shoving it up against the leg of the seat. Still no reaction.

'Nice work.' Deon patted Link on the back.

'And I like your style with the spanner …' Link's eyes glazed over. 'Node says to tie them up and watch out for the bur.'

They checked the tool cupboard for rope. There was none.

Deon reached for the lace curtains and pulled one down. He passed it to Link, who walked up the carriage to tie up the drugged Notz.

'Won't be long, Nifty,' Deon called over his shoulder as he pulled down another curtain to tie up Bob.

Nifty hadn't replied. 'Hey, Nifty, nice hat,' Deon called out a second time. Nifty still didn't answer.

'Use this as a gag.' Link threw a curtain tieback to Deon.

With the two Notz restrained, Link turned his attention to the door that opened to the engine while Deon ran to release his uncle. Nifty was still looking drowsy.

'That drug must've hit you hard, Nifty,' Deon said, as he fought with the two heavy straps buckled across his uncle's chest.

As he released the second strap, Nifty tilted sideways, flopping down onto the leather seat. The strange hat was fastened tightly under his chin, and as he fell, a web of wires and black cables that were connected to it trailed across his body. The wires led to a dark wooden box that lay on the seat at the other side of Nifty's crumpled body.

Deon threw himself across the table and yanked hard at the wires running into the side of the box. His sweaty hands slipped on the cables. He wound the trailing wires around his hand and got a firmer grip. Leaning back and using all his weight, he yanked the wires free.

Convulsing wildly on the seat. Nifty threw his head back then lurched forward, smacking into the edge of the table. Deon lunged and put his arm between Nifty's head and the table. He reached around with the other arm to try and hold his uncle still.

'Link! What the hell is this?' he called.

'What's happening?' Link called from the door.

'I pulled the wires out of the box and he's having a fit or something.'

Nifty made sharp barking, grunting sounds. His face switched between saggy lifelessness and pained grimacing with each yelp. His body continued to jerk and thrash. He looked like a ragdoll being shaken by a dog.

Jumping into the seat next to Nifty, Deon tried to hold his uncle's head still. 'Shh, try and keep still, Nifty. I'm sorry, I just wanted to get that thing off you.' The jerking movements eased slightly, but now a white froth was oozing from Nifty's mouth. Deon's hands shook as he tried to sooth his uncle's spasms. 'Sorry, Nifty,' he rasped. 'Keep still. Please keep still.' Deon could hear his heart drumming in his ears. A hot tear rolled down his cheek. 'Nifty, come on.'

'I did this to him,' Deon said to Link.

Link walked over and crouched next to Deon. 'No, you didn't. That's a mind mill, and it's nasty.'

'What does it do?' Deon asked.

'Extract information.'

'How? And why is it called a mind mill?'

'To get flour from wheat you have to put it through a mill.'

'So you're saying … mind mills *pulverise* the brain to get the information out.'

'It's more of an electrical process, but yeah. While the mill's extracting the info, everything that was stored, all the memories and function, get … ground down.'

'No. No way!' Deon choked out. He could feel tears stinging his eyes, and his breath was coming in rapid, panicked chunks.

'He's only been on it a little while. They can't have gotten in that far yet.' Link leaned over and studied the gauges set into the box. His eyes glazed over. 'Nifty says they've only touched a fraction of his mind so far. He reckons the seizures are just a reaction.'

'So I did cause this when I pulled the wires.'

'Deon, you did the right thing. He's disconnected now, so the milling has stopped. We have to concentrate on getting him back to Node quickly.' Link unstrapped the helmet from around Nifty's chin.

Deon was untangling the mess of wires from around his uncle's arms and leg when the carriage door burst open.

All Out, All Change

The door smacked open against the back of the seat, which shunted against the carriage wall and rattled the small window. The first thing through the door was a wall of stench, a combination of the ooze leaking from the waste tanks perched high on top of the engine and the noxious fumes from the burning poop that was billowing from the engine's smoke stack. The stink shoved up into Deon's nostrils. He coughed and gagged, eyes burning. Through the flood of stinging tears he saw a blurry figure standing on the coupling bridge.

Deon shielded Nifty with his body and tensed; he was ready to face the other Notz.

'Got ya again!'

'Scout?' Deon wiped the stinging tears from his eyes.

'The one and only.' Scout clattered through the narrow doorway and closed the door behind him. 'What's taking so long?'

'It's Nifty.' Deon yanked the last of the wires away. 'He won't wake up.'

'He'll be okay,' Link said, squeezing Deon's shoulder. 'But we need to move him.'

Scout stared at Nifty, who was crumpled on the seat, then drew a quick breath and forced a smile. 'Lifting heavy things is one of my many skills.'

Scout moved in close to Nifty and braced against the back of the leather seat. Deon and Link manoeuvred the dead weight of Nifty's body out from where he lay, half under the narrow table, and hefted him into Scout's arms. Then they all made their way back through the saloon car towards the coupling bridge and the relative safety of the second carriage.

Link froze as he went to cross between the carriages. Deon reached back and guided Link's frozen body inside the second carriage and closed the door behind them.

'Node says we're nearly halfway to the next station,' said Link, blinking. 'There'll be more Notz there. We need to get Nifty off the train and start heading back.'

'Let's go, then,' said Scout, turning towards the rear door with Nifty's limp body in his arms.

'Hey!' came an echoing voice from the first carriage. 'He's gone.'

The train shuddered and decelerated. Scout yanked the door open and ran through to the third car carrying Nifty.

The door at the front of the carriage slammed open and the angry voice boomed, 'Found them!' A man with a red, puffy face lumbered toward them. 'Stinking robot brats!'

Deon turned and backed towards the door, pushing it closed behind him. He tried to create a barrier between Nifty and the Notz. All the doors were open in front of him and he could see all the way back through the train. A fourth Notz, who Deon thought must be the train's driver, was moving across from the engine.

Deon knew he was going to have to fight again, but they had left everything except Nifty behind when they left the first carriage. He scanned around, looking for anything he could use as a weapon. He could see Link doing the same.

Scout burst back in from the last carriage. He slammed the door closed, and shoved Deon and Link sideways. 'Down, now!'

The two boys scrambled for cover behind a seat.

Unlatching a cabinet, Scout's augz fizzed as he pulled on the door, twisting it until the wood creaked and the door ripped from its hinges with a screech of twisting metal. He held the door in front of him as a shield. He slammed his aug frame into the wood and the cracking echoed through the carriage. Then he growled.

Both Notz paused mid-stride.

'Nifty's safe,' Scout mumbled as he thumped his arm on the shield. 'Retro's going up.' He growled again, louder this time.

The train shuddered and lurched. It started losing speed. The red-faced man leaned against the seat and lifted a catapult gun. He pulled back the sling strap and locked it in place. With the driver holding him steady, the man used small metal tongs to carefully place a bur into a clip on the gun. He loaded a second bur from a different tin, but this time didn't use the tongs.

'Do you think that's blue-ring?' Deon whispered, hoping Scout had heard him.

Scout nodded, held the shield up higher, thumped, screeched and started sprinting towards the red-faced man. Deon saw the driver step out through the door behind him. There was a click of the release spring as the gun fired.

Scout was still drumming and growling, so Deon knew he hadn't been hit, but he also knew that the burs could bounce off the shield and land anywhere. If one of those burs knocked him out he'd need carrying home like Nifty. If the blue-ring bur hit him, nothing would happen, but if it landed on Link it would be a different story.

Deon rolled on top of Link to shield him from the burs.

There was a crash of splintering of wood as Scout ploughed into the red-faced man and pushed him towards the half-open door. There was a dull thud, like banging on a bone drum, as the man's head hit the metal door handle. The door slammed shut. The man slid towards the floor with the broken catapult gun pressed into his chest. He lay slumped against the door, drooling and bleeding.

Link was squirming and mumbling underneath Deon.

'Hang on,' Deon said. He hadn't felt anything pierce his skin, but he didn't know how close the burs might be. 'Don't move yet, Link.' He twisted his head around to see where the burs had landed. They lay near each other, close to the opposite wall of the carriage. He pointed them out to Link.

'Thanks for that, mate,' said Link, as he scrambled out from under Deon. He quickly stood, pulled down some lace curtains and moved through the carriage to tie up the red-faced man.

The sound of heavy bounding footsteps echoed down from the roof. There was shouting. Deon recognised Retro and Glide's voices, but the words were undiscernible.

'Thanks, Link,' said Scout. 'Nice knots on the Notz. Three down, one to go.' He shoved the red-faced man with his boot and the man toppled over slowly. Moving his boot to the unconscious man's rump, Scout pushed the dead weight of the third fallen Notz behind the seat to clear the doorway. Then he opened the door and let rip with his most threatening growl.

The weedy train driver was halfway down the first carriage, backing towards the front door. Scout stepped across the coupling bridge towards him. He stopped and stared at the driver, who took another stumbling backward step towards the door and the engine.

Scout advanced, growling. 'Klaato barada nikto,' he yelled.

Robot night. Deon couldn't help smiling.

'Too funny,' said Link, shaking his head.

The driver had backed up against the rear of the engine and seemed frozen there.

Following Scout through the first carriage, Deon and Link stepped over the Notz called Bob, who was unconscious. Deon remembered the heavy spanner he'd left behind. He grabbed it, just in case.

Scout growled once more as he walked forward through the carriage. He stopped for a moment at the table where

Nifty had been sitting. He leaned over and grabbed the heavy mind-mill box by its handle. 'A club to go with my shield,' he said, then stepped through the door and glared at the skinny driver. 'Unlucky you.'

The driver took one last step and backed up against the rear of the engine. His shoulder pushed against something, and his face changed. He didn't look scared anymore. He reached behind and released the catapult gun from its housing on the rear wall of the engine. The gun was loaded with two burs.

Scout glanced up from the loaded gun to a reflection in the small window behind the driver's shoulder. He could see Retro was on the carriage roof, and she was smiling. She signalled that she and Glide would take it from there and waved him off.

'See ya,' said Scout, loud enough for Retro to hear over the engine.

Scout waved at the driver, stepped back inside and slammed the door shut. He grabbed the spanner from Deon's hand and jammed it up between the door handle and the seat, making sure the driver stayed out.

Scout and Deon headed to the rear door. As they crossed to the second carriage, Scout stopped and pointed back over his shoulder. 'I'm curious to see what those two have planned for the driver. You and Link go check on Nifty.'

Deon was heading for the last carriage before Scout had finished the sentence.

On the roof, Retro had seen Glide signal that Scout was coming through. Then she'd heard the robot-like yelling and seen the driver pick up the gun. The train had lost speed when the driver left the engine unattended, but it was still difficult to stay upright on the back deck of the engine when the train swept around a curve.

The driver had braced himself by hooking his arm around the pipe that ran from the waste tank into the furnace. The two burs were seated in the clips, and he was struggling to pull the sling back and lock it into place as the train rocked.

Retro knew she was in full view, but the driver was looking down and hadn't noticed her. She studied the pipe and the rail that ran around the base of the waste tank on the engine's roof. She smiled.

'Yes!' the driver said, after finally hooking the catapult sling in place.

'It's time.' Retro's augz clicked and fizzed as she leapt into the air. She somersaulted across the gap from the carriage to the engine, grabbed the poop tank's support frame, swung her legs out and kicked the pipe hard. It creaked and twisted, and the filthy brown sludge sprayed all over the driver.

He shrieked and flung an arm up to shield himself from the foul rain. But regardless of the foulness, he didn't drop the gun. Retro kept swinging, and let the momentum to carry her up and onto the top of the tank. Now the driver was looking up. As she retreated across the roof and out of his line of fire, he pulled the trigger and launched the burs.

'Ouch,' Glide yelled above Retro.

Below Retro, Scout opened the door. He swung the heavy box at the driver's head. The force of the blow sent the man tumbling from the train in a screeching, effluent-covered tangle of arms and legs. 'All out, all change.' Retro smiled.

Scout leapt back into the carriage and slammed the door shut to escape the sewage fountain.

Sitting on top of the tank, above the foul spray, Retro could see Glide was having problems and knew she had to find a way of stopping the train. She swung over the roof edge and into the driver's cabin. She found the emergency all-stops lever and yanked it on just in time to see her best buddy's arms droop. Glide's wings became sluggish, and she looked terrified. Her wings stopped flapping and she fluttered gracelessly downwards, crumbling into the dry yellow grass beside the railway tracks.

Better Faster Stronger

Deon walked back through the end carriage to where Nifty was lying on one of the leather seats with his eyes half open, seeing nothing. Deon kneeled down between the seats, getting as close to Nifty as he could. His uncle was so still. He squeezed Nifty's hand, then rubbed it and started telling him details of the fight. Nifty stayed still. Deon added some dramatic gestures and sound effects, but Nifty still didn't respond.

Something outside caught Deon's eye. Glide's wings had gone slack and were billowing around her body as she dropped from the sky. *The blue-ring.* A cause-and-effect chain unravelled in his mind.

'Stay with Nifty,' Deon said to Link, and ran to the rear carriage door as the train ground to a chugging stop. Leaning out from the coupling, he saw a pile of wings and bent limbs sticking out of the spikes of yellow grass. The others had also seen Glide and were moving towards her.

Deon theorised that the blue-ring was transmitted by physical contact. When the toxin-covered bur pierced the skin, the virus worked like any other. But what if the virus could be transmitted through skin-to-skin contact? What would happen if one of the others touched her? Deon knew he was immune, but there was a real risk for everyone else.

'Don't touch her!' he screamed, as he jumped down and ran through the grass. 'Don't touch her, it might be the blue-ring.'

Glide lay tangled within her pretzelled wings. She wasn't moving.

Deon skidded in and knelt next to her. 'Hey, Glide, wake up.' He shook her shoulders. He hoped she'd only been hit by the knockout bur, because if it were the blue-ring one, the virus could already be affecting her cyber components. How long before it moved across a connection point and into her blood? The others couldn't risk contact.

The others had heard his warning and hung back, leaning in as closely as they dared.

He leaned over and felt for her pulse. There were two tiny specks of blood on her cheek where the bur had hit her face. Now he could hear random *buzz-clicks* coming from Glide's aug connection points as they misfired. The truth felt like a rock in his guts.

'Her pulse and breathing seem okay.' Deon hesitated, holding his breath for a moment. 'Listen, can you hear her augz … they're fizzing.'

'Tetrodotoxin—over.' Bump sighed.

'We all have to get as far from here as we can, and back to Node as soon as possible,' said Scout urgently. He looked back towards the train and then past it, along the tracks.

A loud growl of thunder rumbled. Green-black storm clouds were rolling in from the east towards the edge of the plateau.

'I'll carry Glide,' said Deon. 'You guys can't touch her. The bur hit her face, but the toxin must've spread on her skin to reach her frame connection points, so it might spread to you as well.'

'Scout!' Link was leaning out of the train door, looking very pale. 'Nifty's not looking so good. Node says we need to get him home fast.'

Scout ran to the carriage. Seconds later, he stood at the carriage door with Nifty's drooping body cradled in his arms.

Deon looked up at his uncle, who seemed smaller somehow. Deon instinctively moved away from Glide and started running towards his uncle, ready to jump up onto the train and see his uncle, hug him.

Cause and effect.

Deon froze. He couldn't get close to anyone now that he'd touched the blue-ring. If he touched Nifty, Scout wouldn't be able to carry him without huge risk; no one would. Deon sagged and huffed out a long sighing breath. He stepped back from the train.

'Nifty will be fine when we get him home,' said Scout.

'How can you be so sure?' Deon said.

'Node said he's handled mind-mill recoveries like this before,' Link said. 'We'll get Nifty home and start fixing this.'

'And then, when he's back on his feet, Nifty and Node will use what they've discovered about the blue-ring to help Glide.' Scout smiled and nodded towards Glide. 'So it looks like it's your turn to do some piggy-backing, Deon.' He jumped down from the carriage with Nifty in his arms. 'We've got to go,' he said, 'will you be okay?'

'I'm good,' Deon said. 'Glide and I will be right behind you.'

Scout offered another half-smile and turned, striding away down the track.

Deon watched Nifty's arms and legs flop and sway with each bounding step Scout took, then he forced himself to turn away and walk back through the grass. Crouching low, he lifted Glide into his arms. She was lighter than he expected. As he stood and adjusted his balance, she groaned and murmured in complaint, which he took as a good sign. He started walking east.

'You sure you're okay to carry her?' Link asked.

'I'll be fine, but slow. Do you think she'll get sicker soon? Doesn't the toxin from a blue-ring octopus sting work fast?'

Link zoned out for a moment then refocused. 'Node says the toxin will ultimately have the same effect, but it's in the form of a virus now so it has an incubation period. She'll be okay until the virus crosses into her bloodstream.'

'How long?' Deon asked.

'He thinks at least a day, maybe two.'

'And then?'

Link shrugged.

'Come on, Link,' said Retro, 'let's head back and see if we can get that electric bike going. Maybe Deon can get a ride home after all.'

'See you soon—over,' said Bump.

Link climbed onto Retro's back, and they bounded back down the tracks towards the station and disappeared over the edge of the plateau.

The weather had turned as nasty as Deon's mood. Black clouds tumbled across the sky as he walked along the tracks. Thunder growled and cracked around him as he shuffled down the slope of the plateau. Not being able to see the ground with Glide in his arms, he stumbled often, fighting to stay upright and avoid dropping her. Then he fell and landed hard on his knees. As he struggled to stand up, the first heavy drops of rain fell. As the ground dampened, a strangely spicy smell of dirt and decay wafted upward.

Now the ground was becoming slick underfoot, and he had to take smaller, shuffling steps. The abandoned bike was up ahead, and Retro and Link were bent over it, talking.

Deon stopped a few metres away, breathing heavily. Gently, he lay Glide down on the soft ferns. He checked her breathing and heart rate, and turned to Link and Retro. 'She seems the same. Can you get the bike going?'

'No luck,' said Retro.

'Where's Bump?' asked Deon.

'He went ahead with Scout,' said Link. 'Catch.' He threw Deon a flask of water.

'What happened?' Deon's body flooded with the heat of panic. 'Is Nifty all right?'

'Sorry,' Link said, 'I didn't mean to scare you. Everything's the same with Nifty. Scout just needed Bump to carry the gear, so they kept going.'

Deon exhaled a shuddering breath. He just wanted Nifty to wake up.

From her bed of ferns, Glide started making wheezing noises.

'Quark!' Deon ran back to her side.

Link followed, but stood back. He stared at Glide for a long moment, and then blinked. 'Node wants to try something he and Nifty have been working on,' he said. 'We're going to go on ahead. Node will give the device to Throttle, and he'll bring it out and meet us up the track to save time. Then we'll double back and bring it to you. Sort of like leapfrogging, but without the jumping.'

'What device?'

'Details later,' said Link, hopping onto Retro's back.

'Follow the wheel tracks, we'll be back as fast as we can,' said Retro. They disappeared along the skinny track and into the wall of green.

Deon was alone. The water from the flask was cool as it flowed down his throat. He hadn't realised how thirsty he was. He forced himself to stop gulping. He offered Glide some water, and she instinctively licked her lips when she felt the cool drops, but coughed and spluttered when he tipped some into her mouth.

Deon slung the flask strap over his shoulder on lifted the wheezing Glide back into his arms. The black skies opened up and released the full force of the storm. He fumbled and slipped down the last of the slope, and they were both soaked through before they reached the partial shelter offered by the rainforest canopy.

Sound travels at three hundred and fifty metres per second. If you count the seconds from the time you see a lightning flash to when you hear the sound, and then divide the number of seconds by three, you know roughly how many kilometres away the lightning strike was.

Deon often found it comforting to lose himself in mathematical calculations. Right now it was helpful. He was walking alone through a massive tropical storm, carrying a girl wearing a metal exoskeleton, which was essentially a lightning rod, so he was happy to be able to monitor the storm, even in this informal way, to see if the lightning was coming closer or moving away. At first he had calculated the storm to be about seven kilometres away. Five lightning flashes later, it was only one kilometre away, and the winds were ripping branches and leaves from the trees and hurling them down all around them.

He realised that if he didn't take shelter soon, he would end up wearing a branch for a hat. So he chose to ignore the science about lightning striking trees and decided to stop, just for a while. He put Glide down in between some large buttressed roots, and sat between her and the rain. He took turns listening to Glide's breathing and doing mental storm calculations until he could count nine seconds between lightning and thunder. Then he picked Glide up again and moved out of the shelter of the tree roots.

He jogged for a while to catch up the time he'd lost, wondering how long Glide could keep wheezing before things got worse. He also kept counting storm seconds in an effort to ignore his burning arms.

Another reason Deon had filled his head with mathematical calculations was in the hope that it would leave no room for him to wonder how things were going with Nifty. It wasn't working. When would Nifty wake up? Would he have to go back to Moran's Cove without his uncle? Or would he carry Nifty back through the scoop and have to explain to his mum that he would never wake up?

Tears made hot runnels down Deon's rain-chilled face. He stopped, wondering if the weight he carried in his heart would cause him to sink into the ground. His lungs heaved as sobs erupted into his throat. Nifty, Glide, his dad, his mates … the grief storm he carried inside him was a thousand times greater than the storm he was walking through.

He pulled himself together and trudged on. At least here in the storm his aloneness had a reason. Back at Moran's Cove, regardless of having his mum and uncle, he was alone. He was considered a freak by the morons that bullied him at school, and he could no longer be who he had been back in the city. He and his dad, his mates and his plans. Then his dad got sick and everything changed. He let out a sobbing growl, 'I miss you, Dad.'

Lightning cracked off in the distance. Deon had forgotten to count.

He couldn't take a broken Nifty back in the scoop. He thought of his dad slipping away. He'd do whatever he had to do to fix his uncle and get him home. The lightning cracked again, definitely further away this time. Deon inhaled a deep shuddering breath. Nifty had too many things in his shed and his head that he hadn't told Deon about yet. He wasn't getting away with the top-secret stuff that easily.

The rain began to ease and the thunder moved further away. Deon could hear Glide's breathing becoming uneven, rasping, laboured.

'Hang in there, Glide. We'll get you back home soon and fix you up so you're be better, faster, stronger.'

He shuffled her up a little higher in his arms and tried to run, but the wet leaves had turned slimy underfoot and he had to slow down again. 'Quark,' he muttered, 'this is taking too long.'

The slipping got worse as the path started sloping downwards. Then he realised the slope meant he was entering the beginning of the valley where the falls and bowers were. Placing Glide down on the ground gently, he allowed himself to stop for a moment. He gulped huge breaths as he checked her pulse and breathing. Regardless of her rasping breath, her pulse still felt as strong as it had back at the train.

Deon offered her a sip of water, which she ignored. He took a quick mouthful himself and choked as he swallowed. Overhead he heard a coughing chitter up in the canopy.

'Rex?' he called. Rex, or whichever quollago it was, answered with a long echoing yowl. A moment later, Deon heard a piercing whistle.

'I told you, Glide, better, faster, stronger, just hang on, okay?' He lifted her and bolted in the direction of the whistle, with Rex racing through the treetops above him.

Throttle appeared in front of him, with Link on his back.

'Stop right there,' Link said, as he jumped down.

'You said you'd have something to help her,' Deon said. Placing Glide back down on the ground, he checked her breathing once more and then shook out his sore arms.

'Catch.' Link threw something small and round. It spun threw the air between them. Deon lunged and caught it.

'Good catch—over,' Bump said, smiling.

The small metal disc had two flashing lights that strobed at varying speeds, at a ratio of six to one.

'Hold it to the base of her skull, really low, just at the top of her spine.' Link pointed out the position on himself. 'Hold it there and press hard, until you hear a click.'

Deon positioned the disc and pressed hard. There was a click and a weak whimper from Glide.

'That moan is a good sign,' said Link.

'So what is this thing?' said Deon, looking at the flashing lights again.

'Node calls it an autonomic stimulator,' said Link.

'So it's regulating her heart and breathing?'

'Yep, the blue-ring toxin—'

'Tetrodotoxin—over.'

'—the toxin would eventually have shut down her breathing. Now we can keep those signals going until we can get home and put her on life support. With time, her body should break down the toxin on its own.'

'Need a lift—over.'

Throttle unloaded something from Bump's back. He pushed it towards Deon then backed away.

'Unreal,' Deon said, looking at the half-sled, half-wheelbarrow. He lifted Glide into it and turned for home.

The Cave

The falls were wild again after the storm. Water rushed over each rock step and plummeted downward, turning each pool below into a blender. The racing flow of the creek churned the air in the narrow valley, creating a cool, moist breeze that swirled down the valley and twisted up into the narrow gap in the trees above the falls.

Deon breathed in the coolness, exhaling with a shudder of relief. He was out from the muggy heat that had gathered under the forest canopy after the storm. Better than that, he was here, finally, and not alone. Now everything would be fixed.

'Node said to bring her straight up—over.' Bump turned and headed up a narrow path next to the falls.

'Up where?'

Bump didn't answer. He was just doing his Bump thing, bending plants and pushing fallen branches aside to widen the narrow track to make room for Glide's wheelbarrow. The track was steep and slippery. Deon pushed upwards along a thin zigzag of muddy trail that was overhung by the dense green. This track was not visible from lower down in the valley. His arms ached and his legs were shaking under him. Now the moist air swirling up from the falls was making him extra sweaty.

The track finally ended. They were at the top of the steps. The track appeared to stop at the rock wall. Ahead of Deon, Bump turned abruptly and disappeared, walking right into the water pouring over the falls. Deon balked. Bump had augz to handle walking through the deluge, but he didn't, and Glide certainly wouldn't handle it.

'Right turn—over.' Bump reappeared from under the falls. He was still dry, and was waving Deon forward.

Deon followed, threading the wheelbarrow along the narrow ledge of rock that was hidden behind the rushing curtain of water.

Bump accelerated to full speed, running directly at a craggy fold in the rock, and disappeared again. Deon stopped and stared, then pushed the wheelbarrow closer. As he angled around the path, he saw that the rock face creased in on itself, creating huge folds. The creases were deep, and he leaned in, staring into the shadows until the folded rock revealed its hidden passage. He pushed the wheelbarrow into the narrow gloom of the tunnel. No wonder no one could find this place, he thought. The wheelbarrow scraped along the rough walls as he squeezed it through the narrow blackness.

Glide groaned weakly.

'Sorry, Glide.' He slowed down, waiting for his eyes to adjust to the darkness.

Ahead was a vertical snake of watery light that reflected off Glide's augz frame. The tunnel widened and the damp, uneven ground became smooth underfoot. Deon sniffed. The temperature had dropped dramatically and the air had a … robotic smell. It smelled of circuits and solder, which reminded him of his Robot Team Challenge days.

He could hear voices up ahead.

The snake of light broadened as he came around the last bend and light filled the end of the tunnel. He stopped, shook his tired arms and stared around. The left side of the tunnel opened out and became a wall that reached high into a vaulted space in front of him. He stepped far enough forward to see beyond the tunnel and up into the expanse of the cave. The light revealed uneven striations in the folds of rock.

His breath caught as he saw stalactites hanging down from the almost-darkness where the light struggled to reach. The glistening rocky icicles looked like immense dragon teeth. He stopped and stared, releasing a long breath. There was so much he wanted to ask right now.

'Welcome to the bat cave—over.'

Glide groaned.

'I don't think she liked the joke, Bump,' said Deon. He pushed the wheelbarrow closer to the rock wall to ensure that no one would touch it until it could be scrubbed clean, or maybe burned. He lifted Glide into his arms. As he did, he added a few hundred questions to his unanswered-question list, but he asked only one of them. 'Where do you want me to put her?'

Link appeared from the shadows at the back of the cave. 'We've set up an isolation room for her.' He pointed to the second of two glass cubicles on the other side of the cave.

In the first cubicle, Nifty was lying on a bed. Wires, and what looked like the mind-mill cap, covered his head. He was staring up at the dragon teeth in the dark reaches of the cavern without blinking. Deon's knees buckled. He squeezed out a shuddering sigh, and carried Glide across the cave. He stopped and looked through the glass at Nifty; his uncle's face looked like a deserted house.

'Why is he wearing a mind mill?' he snapped.

'It's not a mind mill,' Link said. 'It's sort of the reverse, a partial link to the plexus to help with his recovery.'

'How safe is it?'

'Just a monitor, really, one hundred percent safe,' Link hurried to say. 'He's better than he looks. He's breathing fine, everything's good … he just won't come back to us yet. Node says Nifty's probably waiting for you, and when he hears you he'll come good and have plenty to say.'

Deon straightened his tired shoulders and stood tall. 'Where should I put Glide?'

'On that bed, I'll go suit up and get her onto the life support. The antiviral's ready to trial, but it's a vaccine so it's no use to her now. Good news, the old medical files tell us that her body will break down the toxin in time. This machine will be her heart and lungs while she works on the poison.'

163

Deon lay Glide gently on the bed, looking across to Nifty and then back to Link. 'Be careful, okay? Don't get sick.'

'I will, and I won't,' said Link, as he slipped into a plastic suit that looked like a costume from a B-grade, plague-apocalypse movie. 'The suit is top notch,' he said, 'nothing can get inside. When Glide's up and about, I'll get her to scrub with this nasty stuff.' He held up an orange tube. 'It kills everything, so don't get it into your mouth or eyes, okay?' He tossed the tube to Deon. 'Showers are back there, near the door. Scrub up and then go wake up your lazy uncle.' Link smiled. 'He's been sleeping long enough.'

Judging by the choking fumes and the burning sensation on his skin after the shower, Deon was sure he didn't have a microbe alive on him anywhere. He'd dressed in the embarrassing bike pants and T-shirt that had been left for him while he'd been scrubbing.

He hurried straight to Nifty's glass cubicle. It was stark, with a bed in the centre and an array of operating-room equipment against the walls. He was relieved to see that his uncle didn't need anything like Glide's life support.

'Hi, Nifty,' Deon said, 'hey, why won't you wake up?'

Fuse answered his question instead, but it wasn't really Fuse. His eyes were glazed, and he was standing rigidly in the door of the cubicle. His hands were frozen on the handles of a trolley that held fruit and sandwiches. 'Hang in there, Deon, he'll wake up,' said a voice that didn't belong to Fuse.

'Node?' Deon gulped.

'Yeah … and no. Anyway, I'm pleased to finally meet you,' said Node-Fuse. 'It's a shame it couldn't have been under more festive circumstances, but thank you for bringing Glide back to us.'

Deon stared into Fuse's face, now robbed of expression. His unanswered questions started leaking out. 'While we're talking like this, tell me what's happening to Fuse.'

'The brainiacs kindly let me borrow them when I need to move around, or do an augz install, or take care of your uncle, that sort of stuff. It's kind of like a nap for them.'

'But what … where are you?' Deon scanned the room for wires or some place that could be the connection for Node, but saw nothing he recognised as a link.

'I'm here. I'm sort of all around the cave and out in the plexus.' Node gestured with Fuse's stiff arms. 'I'll explain it all later, but right now I want you to eat. Then you can bug Nifty with stories and questions until he wakes up and tells you to shut up. Got it?'

Before Deon could ask any more questions, Node had released Fuse and disappeared back to where ever he—it—really was.

'Deon, huge effort on the recovery,' Fuse said, sounding like Fuse again. 'Kudos, mate. How are your arms feeling? The bouncers forget how we feel after a physical challenge like that without any augz. You must be hungry.' He pushed the trolley closer.

The sweet, tangy smell of the fruit reached Deon's nose and his stomach growled. His mouth watered, but he looked back at his sleeping uncle. 'Maybe I should eat after I've tried to wake Nifty.'

'Come on, do both at once. And chew with your mouth open, maybe that'll annoy him awake.' Fuse shoved the food under Deon's nose and left him alone in the glass cubicle.

'Thanks, Fuse.' He devoured some fruit, and watched Link and Fuse talking in the other cubicle as he started on a sandwich. Link appeared to be checking readouts on the monitors, and Fuse seemed to be asking questions about Glide. Deon couldn't hear what they were saying, but Link's gestured answers looked positive enough.

Deon relaxed and concentrated on the rest of the sandwich, feeling proud that he had brought Glide back and saved her life. Next, he would nag Nifty back to consciousness. He smiled and continued to watch Fuse and Link through the glass wall. They both glazed and froze for a moment, and Deon knew they were talking to Node.

Then they blinked and were back again. Both looked towards Deon, nodding, shrugging, their gestures looking less positive now. They saw him looking their way and were suddenly all smiles and thumbs-up. Deon finished his last mouthful of sandwich and felt like he was swallowing a rock.

Three hours passed as Deon related every family story he could remember, from prize nights and his mum's graduation from her arts course to family holidays. He retold his versions of Nifty's surprise reveals of inventions over the years, when they were no longer top secret. The only thing he didn't talk about was his dad getting sick.

Now he was pulling out the big guns to make Nifty really think. 'How cool is this cave, anyway? When we get back home, to our time, I mean, we should hike up here and leave an object in this cave.'

Nifty didn't move or blink.

'Do you remember when you told me about the bootstrap paradox? In a way, all this is sort of like that paradox. Let's decide right now what to leave. I know, that old shoe of mine you kept from my first race win. Mum and Dad kept one and so did you. Let's decide where to leave it. How about up there, in that deep rock crevice? When we're back in our time, we'll bring the shoe here and hide it.'

A cause-and-effect cyclone hit Deon's mind. His heart thumped. Maybe the shoe was already here. If he looked to see if the shoe was here then he would know the future; he would know if Nifty was going to be all right. If the shoe was here, that meant Nifty would get better and they would go home and go hiking. They'd find the cave and hide the shoe.

Deon stood and almost ran across the cave. He leapt at the wall, grabbed the edge of the rock shelf and dug his toe into a tiny fold in the rock. The crevice was full of shadows. He stretched his arm inside until he felt his shoulder click, reaching into the limits of the dark space. There was no shoe.

He dropped back to the floor and pressed his face against the cool wall. Hot tears tracked down his chilled skin.

He had needed that shoe to be there so badly. He crumpled and sat on the cave floor. After a few minutes, he pulled up his T-shirt and wiped his wet face.

When he looked up, Fuse was standing, face glazed, in front of him. 'Were you looking for this?' came Node's voice. Fuse was holding a small, worn shoe covered in grass stains. The faded remains of the word BANKS was written on the side.

Deon gasped, then laughed. His mum labelled everything. He scrambled to his feet. 'We did it!' He grabbed the shoe and squeezed it hard into his chest. It was real. 'He'll be okay, Nifty will be okay. How did you know where it was?'

Node paused longer than usual when working through a brainiac. 'It's not that big a cave … and I did some renovations in here.' Fuse gave a marionette shrug on Node's behalf.

'We put the shoe here,' Deon said, 'so that means Nifty and I have been here in the past, or we'll be here sometime in our future, which is sometime in your past. And because we did do it, that means that Nifty should be awake. But he's not.'

Deon was confused. He felt a wave of dizziness. A thought struck him. Maybe he had come here on his own, and the shoe was a memorial. He glared at Fuse's eyes, which were being borrowed by Node. 'None of this would have happened to Nifty if you hadn't brought him here. So what are you doing to fix this?'

Node's voice sounded softer now. 'We're working on another theory about Nifty's condition.'

'Is he dying?'

'No, Deon, not at all,' Node-Fuse said. 'We'd like to try something else to help him recover fully.'

'What? When are you going to do it?' Deon's head was spinning, and he swayed unsteadily.

'We need to do a bit more preparation, so we'll get started in a few hours.'

'What will you do?'

'I'll explain later. I think you've had enough for one day.' Node-Fuse put an arm around Deon's shoulders and steered him back towards Nifty's bed. 'You need some sleep. When we're ready we'll wake you and tell you all the details. You can help us with the procedure if you're willing to.'

'Of course, I'll do anything to help Nifty.'

'Okay. For now, what you have to do is climb onto your lazy uncle's bed and get some rest. Your snoring might wake him. If there's any change, you'll be the first to know.'

'I don't snore,' Deon lied, as he lay down next to Nifty on the narrow bed.

Fuse walked out of the cubical, closing the door.

The glass walls slowly turned opaque and the room dimmed to darkness around him. He rolled onto his side, laid his arm across Nifty's chest and squeezed him tightly. 'Come back, Nifty,' he whispered. 'Huggy-hug-hug-hug.' Deon lay in the dark, listening for any sign that his uncle was coming back. There was just the quiet sighs of Nifty's breathing. Then sleep overtook him.

Brainiac

Light pried at Deon's eyelids. He could hear quiet singing. '…hmm-hmm-hmm things hmm-hmm-hmm say to you hmm-hmm-hmm-hmm…'

'Nifty?'

'No, mate, it's just me, us,' said Node, talking through Link this time.

'But I thought I heard one of Nifty's songs from his nineties playlist.'

'Um … you were probably having a dream.'

'I can't believe I even slept.' Deon sat up and looked at Nifty's chest slowly rising and falling. His uncle didn't seem to have moved a micron since the lights were dimmed. 'Have you made all your preparations? When do we start?'

'Soon. Have some food first.' Node-Link pushed a trolley of food towards Deon.

'When we talked before … through Fuse,' Deon said as he ate, 'you said you had a theory about what's happening to Nifty. Tell me about it.'

'Okay,' said Node-Link. 'Sometimes people…brainiacs, get their personalities tangled up inside the plexus and can't find their way out again.'

'What's that got to do with Nifty? He's not a brainiac.'

'Essentially, the mind mill was trying to take Nifty into the plexus and store his information. When that happened, I think his personality might have been drawn in.'

'Into where?'

'Into the plexus.'

'How does that work?'

'The plexus was created by making connections between human minds to replace the old silicone circuits of the internet in your time. You know how real a dream can feel. Well, imagine being inside something that contains the dreams and thoughts of many minds.'

'So what's the program? How's it coded?'

'It's essentially made of everything you know about your own life, and some bits from other people's memories and information. It's an easy place to get lost, especially if you don't really know what it is. Imagine being lost in the woods and not realising you're lost so you can't look for the trail to follow to get out.'

'So Nifty's mind is wandering in some plexus underworld, maybe not even knowing he should be looking for a way out.'

'In theory, yes.'

'Did he get stuck in there because of what I did … when I ripped all the wires off?' Deon felt his food bubbling in his stomach like some sour poison.

'Deon, it was not your fault. We've lost plenty of minds in the plexus, and we've also rescued plenty.'

'So send someone to get him. Why haven't you gone looking for him already? Aren't you like a supercomputer or something?' Deon shook his head. He was running out of words to articulate his thoughts in this context.

'Yes, connecting to the plexus is easy for me. I had a lot to do with its design and I sort of … I suppose you could say I inhabit it. That's the easiest way to get the concept.'

'So off you go, find Nifty and bring him back.' Deon felt the heat of resentment rising in him. 'He'd never have been in this position if you hadn't scooped him and brought him here to help you. You owe him.'

'I know the debt I owe to you both, but there was no other way to get the help I needed to save the Havz from the blue-ring.' Link's puppet shoulders sagged. 'I had no one else to lean on. Nifty was the only one who could give me what I needed.'

'Well, now he needs you.' Deon clenched his hands into tight fists. He blew out a long, hard breath and willed his hands and the rest of him to relax. 'Let's focus on solving the problem.'

'Right,' said Node-Link, staring into Deon's eyes. 'The plexus is made up of lots of minds working, learning, playing. Some shouldn't be there, so they're hiding. The problem is that some of the minds might recognise us before we can discover anything about Nifty's location.' Node-Link placed his hands on Deon's shoulders. 'We need to send someone into the plexus who is unknown.'

'Me? Is that what you wanted me to help with?'

'It sure is.'

'But don't you have to have the connection? Would I have to be auged, like Link, like Fuse?'

'Yes, that's what you would have to do, if you were willing.'

'Of course, I'll do anything to help Nifty. But why would I be able to do it, to search in the plexus, when you guys can't?'

'New brainiacs don't have a history inside. Once they've been there a while, they leave mental residue, tattered pieces of dreams and memories that others can use to recognise them or twist to use against them. You won't have any of that, so you should be next to invisible inside the plexus.'

'Invisible, but also horribly lost. I'm guessing there won't be any maps to help me find my way around.' Deon shook his head.

'The plexus is intuitive. It will scan your data…sorry, memories, and set up a personal-context landscape you will understand. It'll probably feel like you're moving through somewhere familiar, except the whole place will have a dream-like quality, and there'll be odd, out-of-context things poking into your scape from other users.'

'It sounds dangerous. How will I defend myself or Nifty if I need to?'

'Be a coder.'

'H-how would that work?' stammered Deon.

'The plexus is a richly creative environment. It'll respond to your ideas in a cause-and-effect way.'

'Meaning?'

'Cogito ergo sum.'

'I think, therefore I am.'

'That's how it works inside the plexus. If you can think up an action, a reaction, a solution that fixes the situation, it'll take form and be implemented. But …'

'But?'

'All other users have the same power to create stuff as you do.'

'Comforting news,' Deon said, rolling his eyes. 'Thanks for the snack-sized guide to the plexus, but I'm not a brainiac.'

Node-Link drew a deep breath and blew it out slowly. He held out his hand and opened it. In the centre of his palm was a flat shiny disc. At a point on the edge of the disc sat a cluster of coloured filaments.

'Is that it? Is that what will make me auged? It's tiny.'

'So is the bluetooth in your phone. It works in kind of the same way. Once it's implanted, the filaments will be activated to grow, and they'll link in with the related regions of your brain to create a two-way interface between you and the plexus.'

'How long does it take the connections to grow and link up?'

'Usually a few hours.'

'We don't have a few hours.'

'So you're willing to be auged?'

'I've already told you, I'd do anything for Nifty.'

'That's what I thought, so …'

Realisation dawned on Deon. 'You already did it.'

Node-Link nodded slowly, and indicated for Deon to touch the back of his neck. There was a dressing patch covering an area that felt slightly tender when he touched it. 'It will not, ever, be activated without your permission, but I felt I knew your mind well enough to take a chance and do it while you slept to save time.'

'Switch it on.' Deon grabbed Link's arm. 'I want to go find Nifty.'

For the next hour, Deon fumbled around in the plexus with guidance from Node, or at least a shadowy version of Node, which seemed to keep itself off on the fringes and just out of Deon's direct perception.

At first, being in the plexus felt like walking backwards, blindfolded, through a noisy disco during an earthquake. Deon's context landscape was a selection of favourite spots from his old neighbourhood in the city, blended with the environs of Moran's Cove, including his new high school. The worst thing was seeing Johno and some of the zombie morons in the distance, waxing their boards.

Node had instructed him to just wander around, get familiar with the landscape and try to get over the feeling of travel sickness and vertigo that came with being a new brainiac. By the time they withdrew from the plexus, Deon was feeling confident. He was finally free of the tilting nausea, and he was starving. 'Better, faster, stronger,' he whispered to himself. He touched the back of his neck and shuddered.

The Plexus

Entering the plexus for the second time was less unnerving for Deon and made more sense. Instead of stumbling through a fog and slowly realising that he was in a dreamed-up Moran's Cove like he had the first time, he was aware of where he was, and although the scape was still dreamlike, it felt more familiar and the dizzying nausea did not return.

Deon realised that whatever part of his brain was creating his scape had adapted quickly and was taking full advantage of the rules, or lack of them. He jolted as the conjured scene took shape and he realised he was seeing Moran's Cove from above. He was flying across the treetops, and past the broken power pole southwest of town.

His stomach lurched as he swooped down along the plexus version of the road and landed lightly halfway down the hill. He could feel his feet touch the road, but as soon as they did, all his other senses were skewed. The scene looked wrong. He knew this was supposed to be the long, straight familiar road leading back to town that he'd spent endless hours running along, but right now it was folded in on itself like a fractal. It was like being inside some weird, world-sized kaleidoscope.

Five black ribbons of road all converged in the centre of Deon's vision. Multiple copies of trees and power poles were bent and leaning inward, as if they were being pulled into the pinpoint of a black hole. Deon felt his stomach squelch and his face flood with heat as the dizziness and nausea returned. Was he really upside down? He stumbled and gasped, trying to grip the ground with his feet.

Concentrate with all your senses equally, advised Node's disembodied voice from somewhere behind him. *You're focusing too much on the visual at the moment, so the plexus is manifesting a very dense scape.*

Deon took a deep breath. He smelt the dry muskiness of the dead grass clumped around the fence posts and the dust that kicked up when he ran on the shoulder of the road. His head started to clear. Now there were only three roads in his vision and a faded blue sky was unfolding overhead. He could hear birds now, crows complaining as they flew across the expanding, unfolding sky and landed on the now upright trees. His stomach calmed as this newly created scape stopped tilting and threatening to throw him sideways.

'Let's get going,' said Deon, turning to look directly at the shadowy half-presence of Node.

I can't go with you, not fully, I'll skew your scape and be noticed.

'How will I know where to go? The plexus is your place. You'd be the perfect guide. Are you sure you can't come?'

I know it's weird and hard for you to understand, but I can't actually be in the plexus because the plexus is in me.

'Yeah, you're right, that is weird and hard to understand.'

I am Node. All the connections for the plexus go through me. I can dabble a little in the scapes, but it's mostly like visiting my own mind in a dream, or maybe meditation.

'You said the plexus is organic because it's created from all the linked brainiacs' brains, but they connect through you. So you must have organic components, too. How big are you? Where are you?'

Such great questions, and such a limited time to answer them. Organic? Somewhat. Big? Yes. Where? Mostly in the cave.

'So …' Deon turned towards Node's shadowy form.

Deon, you're here to find Nifty. Detailed enquiry into my nature can come later, okay?

'And you really can't come with me?'

Really.

'How will I find him?'

You created this scape, Deon. It's your town, and Nifty's town as well. You should go and look for him where you would look for him if you were at home for real. Node's ghostly outline bled into the scape and then it was gone.

Deon stared out at the wavering version of the world he had created. When he had searched for Nifty after they were scooped into this time, Nifty had left him a trail to follow. With luck, Nifty had left another trail for him, if he'd been able to.

179

But the first time, Nifty had had bits and pieces of equipment in his pockets. What would he have now that he was no longer in their time? What would he think to leave, when the world could be anything he chose to create? Deon wondered if he'd even recognise the objects Nifty might leave.

Jogging toward town, he scanned the scape for any sign that Nifty had passed through the same plexus pathways in *his* version of this place. He fell into a steady, comforting rhythm as he jogged down the hill, heading for the unreal showgrounds. Scanning left and right in time with his breathing as he ran.

So many things about Nifty were secret—except how he felt about Deon. A shuddering sigh broke the rhythm of Deon's breathing. Nifty had to be okay. He shook the doubt and fear from his mind, pushed his legs harder and ran on.

Turning at the showgrounds, he headed into this ghostly version of Moran's Cove. The next two streets were deserted, which made sense. Deon hadn't known many people around town, so he couldn't add them to his scape. There were Johno and the surf zombies, of course, but they were the last people he wanted to see in *any* version of Moran's Cove.

There was no sign of a trail from Nifty, unless he had already missed it. An anxious flush of heat crossed his face. He had to keep positive about Nifty. His mind was creating this place, so negative thoughts might become negative … who knew what. Stressing out wouldn't help him create what he needed.

Let's see how this plexus works, he thought. He slowed down and thought a single word: *Skateboard.*

A second later, he was gliding along the smooth street on a small blue fibreglass deck. He pushed off on the road with his right foot and did an ollie. He smiled. Now all he needed was a better skateboard.

He looked down, and the ordinary blue board with its crackling wheels had been replaced by a large wooden deck running on trucks that zinged within the spinning polyurethane of the wheels as he glided down the road. He pushed off again, and did a one-eighty. He laughed. He was so much better on a board in this scape, where the effects of gravity were not a variable, than he had ever been in his time.

Curiosity tempted Deon to experiment further, to see what was really possible in his scape. *Ramp.* The ramp appeared on the road ahead. He pushed hard to gain speed, hit the ramp, did a grab and landed, still upright, on the road. 'Smooth,' he said aloud.

Something flashed in the corner of his vision. He did a quick kick-turn and stopped, flicking the nose of the board up and grabbing it. Then he remembered where he was and let the board go; he could make anything he wanted here in the scape. The board vanished before it hit the road.

He couldn't resist doing a quick audit of the unexpected things he had created in the scape so far: dead grass that changed to green grass, a cool skateboard, an instant skate ramp, and the ability to fly.

The flash he had seen was not something he had created, or at least he didn't think he had created it. Why would he? Maybe it was something from Nifty. He walked a few steps back up the road to where he had seen the glint of light. There it was again, something in the grass at the side of the road.

He parted the lush grass and found a shining plastic disc. One of Nifty's playlist CDs. Deon's heart was pounding. 'Yes!' He held the CD above his head and ran in a tight victory circle around the clump of grass. Of *course* Nifty would leave his songs as a trail. His head was full of them, and they were always leaking out as mumble-hums. And if Nifty was aware of his actions, he'd know the songs wouldn't have any meaning to anyone who saw them in the scape except Deon.

Problem. Round objects weren't helpful for pointing the way. Deon looked down the road, and saw a glint from another CD. If Nifty had left the discs close enough together, Deon wouldn't need to figure out which direction to take. Nifty had an endless supply of songs in the crazy playlist he kept inside his head so Deon knew he could make an endless trail.

Stepping back onto a third, and even more superior, skateboard with one smooth action, he pushed down to the next CD. He stopped and scanned around for the next marker.

'If Nifty can think to leave a trail,' he muttered, 'why can't he find his way out?' He shrugged. He knew he'd be lost here too, if it weren't for the coaching Node had given him before he came into the plexus.

Now that Deon felt more confident about being able to find Nifty, he wanted to do a quick test of the limits of his ability to create things inside the scape.

Unicycle.

The skateboard morphed, and Deon felt the seat of the unicycle that appeared under his butt. He wobbled, then straightened up and pedalled on, sitting high on the unicycle with the breeze blowing in his hair.

He was sure it would only be a matter of time before he found Nifty at the end of his trail of shiny breadcrumbs. Maybe he didn't even need the trail. Nifty had probably taken himself home. Deon pushed down on the pedals of his newly manifested unicycle and rode towards the next glinting CD.

At the next marker, he pedalled back and forth to keep his balance as he looked up the street for the next disc. There were no more markers up ahead so he turned the corner. His hunch was right; it looked like Nifty was heading home.

He rode on, looking down at the unicycle with admiration, wondering how long it would have taken to learn to ride a unicycle outside the plexus.

He slammed into an imposing steel-mesh fence, groping for a handhold to keep from falling. What was this huge fence doing in Moran's Cove, in his scape? Deon pushed himself back off the fence. The unicycle disappeared and he dropped to the ground. He stood rubbing the diamond-shaped dents from his face.

Hoverbike

Through the fence, a wide expanse of grey-black asphalt stretched out in all directions. The field of tar was peppered with endless large metal-clad sheds arranged in rows that stretched out until they faded into a distant vanishing point. Halfway along the central line of sheds, Deon could see that the seventh huge shed was decorated with CDs, lots of CDs. They were threaded onto string and spinning in the breeze, reflecting sparks of light in all directions.

'Nifty!' This must be his scape layering over Deon's. It was probably a version of the army base Nifty had spent so much time at before he retired.

Deon stepped back and looked up and down the length of the fence for a gate. He could see one in the distance, partway along the adjacent fence. It was too far to walk.

Gate. Nothing happened. *Gate*, he suggested more firmly. Nothing. Then he realised that since it was Nifty's scape that was why he was having no success hacking it. He had no choice but to climb over.

No matter how hard he tried to shove his size-eleven running shoes into the diamond-shaped gaps, the fence's mesh was too small for him to get a firm foothold. Maybe he couldn't hack Nifty's scape but he could add a little something of his own.

Ladder.

'Yes!' A long silver extension ladder appeared, leaning against the fence. Deon grabbed the ladder and shook it, testing its sturdiness. He was still amazed at how real everything seemed. He scaled the ladder quickly and swung over the top, ready to lower himself down as best he could.

That's when the air was filled with an ear-splitting screech and the sirens started wailing. Then came distant shouts and the clatter of what Deon dreaded were soldiers mobilising to defend against an intruder. *He* was that intruder. Maybe that's why Nifty hadn't come back. Maybe he was being held inside this compound.

The sirens cut off, but the thunder of boots and shouting came closer. Deon had to get Nifty. He knew he would do badly in any kind of fight. He'd had only had one fight in his life, with the Notz on the train, and he had closed his eyes before he hit the man with the spanner. Even when Johno and the surf zombies had turned on him, he never fought, he just ran. Running right now would get him close to Nifty.

He took off towards the central alleyway that led to the decorated shed, hoping he was right.

'Stop!' one of the soldiers boomed after him. 'One warning only!'

Deon heard a fiery spit from behind him and felt the bullet rush past above his head. His heart thumped as if it might break free from his chest. 'Come on, Nifty, what the hell kind of scape is this?' he muttered. He felt like an actor, specifically the unnamed red uniform in *Star Trek*, the one that got shot before anyone found out what his name was.

Another shot. It skimmed closer this time.

He told himself to run, but then he remembered Node's advice: be a coder, create the scape, and solve the problem.

Hoverbike.

He was airborne in a moment, and everything around him became a blur of speed. He leaned forward and groped for the controls of his impossible but very welcome hoverbike, taking it all in instantly. The handlebars were shiny bronze, with a cluster of gauges in the centre. The engine or whatever was powering the bike made a growling, sucking, blowing sound, and Deon could feel the power coming up through the seat beneath him. I *love* the plexus, he thought.

Another shot was fired, and he heard it ricochet. Sparks sprayed off the wall of the building he sped past. He swung the bike hard to the left. It grazed the corner of a shed and bounced off with a screech of sparks like some out-of-control bumper car. He failed to pull his leg out of the way in time, and when he slammed it into the wall, burning pain flared in his foot. He corrected the bike and then turned sharp right at the end of the building. At least he was safe from the bullets for now.

Waves of pain travelled up his leg. None of this was real, so how could he be hurt? Then he remembered Glide talking about her brother dying inside the plexus. The pain felt so real. Deon gritted his teeth and counted the metal buildings as he sped along the strip of tar. He could hear the guards shouting and running. Soon he'd have to turn right again and cross the central road—and the line of fire—to get to Nifty's shed. He'd counted five sheds; he would need to turn soon.

Each shed had a large roller door and a smaller door for easy access. The roller door on Nifty's shed had not been open. He hoped the small door would be wide enough for a hoverbike to fit through.

At the corner of the seventh shed he slowed the bike for a moment, looking across at Nifty's shed. Roller still closed, smaller door barely open. He lined up the bike with the shed door, which looked so small right now. He poured on the power. The bike hissed and lurched forward. As Deon came into sight crossing the central road, he heard a renewed storm of shouting and guns firing. There was a thudding jolt as a bullet hit the engine, and the hoverbike immediately started to moan and cough.

Deon aimed the bike at the narrow, slightly ajar door and slammed it open with the front of the bike. As he came through the door, the wide handlebars clipped the doorframe and the bike tilted, flinging Deon through the air.

The bike bounced once, scraping across the concrete floor, and they both slid to a stop in front of an alarmed-looking Nifty.

'Deon! What are you doing here?' Nifty said. 'How did you get here? How do you even know where here is?'

'Hi, Nifty, great to see you.' Deon picked himself up off the floor, ran back to the dented door, shouldered it closed and locked it.

'How can you be here?' Nifty stammered again. 'You can't be here.'

Deon realised Nifty didn't know this place wasn't real. 'Do you like my hoverbike?' he said, deciding it was the best way to get Nifty wondering and questioning.

'There are no such things as hoverbikes,' Nifty protested.

'Anything seems possible here in the plexus, that's how I'm here.'

'Plexus?'

'Hey, how long has it been since you retired from active duty with the army and moved to Moran's Cove?'

'That was …' Nifty looked around the shed as if seeing it for the first time.

Unicycle. Deon started riding in lazy circles around Nifty.

'What's going on?' Nifty sputtered.

Skateboard. Deon carved around Nifty, did a kick-turn and stopped, staring at him.

There was shouting and fists pounding on the other side of the door.

'Who's that?' Nifty said.

'The soldiers you have on duty to guard you. They've been shooting at me.' *Unicycle*. Deon circled his uncle again. 'How's your head feeling, Nifty?'

'What?' Nifty lifted his hand to his head and felt the remains of the tattered leather helmet with its wires dangling around his shoulders.

The shouting was louder now, and there was hammering on the door's lock.

'You need to tell them to stand down,' Deon said. 'Call them off.'

Nifty stared at Deon, running his hands through the wires. He tried to remove the cap, but it seemed stuck. The door was buckling.

'Huggy-hug-hug-hug,' said Deon, flinging himself at Nifty and hugging him hard.

Nifty shuddered and drew a huge breath. 'At ease!' he boomed at the soldiers on the other side of the buckling door. His voice had authority and menace that Deon had never heard before. The banging stopped. 'Return to your posts.'

All was quiet. Deon smiled. Nifty was coding his scape without realising it.

Deon clung to Nifty, who wrapped his arms around his nephew and started bouncing around in a stilted version of a huggy-dance circle. 'Huggy-hug-hug-hug,' he mumbled. Then he took a deep shuddering breath and collapsed to the floor, panting. 'What is going on?'

Not willing to let go of Nifty for a moment, Deon sat with him on the floor and told him the unbelievable story of what had happened. Nifty gasped and nodded as Deon's words allowed him to reconnect with the clouded-over memories that the mind mill had tried to steal from him. Deon gave him the snack-sized explanation of the plexus—as he understood it so far.

'Node had explained a bit of that to me,' Nifty said, 'when we were working on the blue-ring antiviral and the autonomic st—'

'It worked, by the way,' Deon interrupted. 'The stim works. Glide got shot with a blue-ring dart when we rescued you from the train, but she's going to be fine and all because of you and Node.'

'Node and I are getting to undo a really bad thing that I started here, all those years ago when I was still in the army.' Nifty drew a shaky breath. 'I'm so glad I got to right that wrong.'

'That's probably why your scape was this place, because your mind came back here to where it all started.'

'Where is your scape?'

'The Cove.'

'Not the city?' Nifty said. 'I know you miss it.'

'Yeah, I do, but I thought you'd be here—there—at Moran's Cove, so that's where I went. Then I crossed into your scape.'

As they spoke, the walls of the shed melted away, and in their place was the familiar purposeful clutter of Nifty's shed, complete with one of his playlist favourites playing through the wall speakers. They walked outside and looked around at the scape version of Moran's Cove.

'All we need to do now is …' Deon realised he wasn't sure how to get out of the plexus. 'I guess we head back across town to the pole on the hill. That's where I first appeared when Node put me into the plexus.'

In the distance was the sound of shouting. Deon hadn't thought about there being anyone else in the plexus, but of course there could be. Maybe he'd been in it long enough to be drawing attention to himself, or maybe they were looking for Nifty. And now he and Nifty were outside the fenced compound, and they were unprotected.

'We should get going then,' said Nifty. 'It wouldn't take us long to get to the pole on one of those hoverbikes of yours.'

'I think the hoverbike might've made me too noticeable, and Node said being noticed isn't a good thing in here.'

'Okay, then let's go for a run,' said Nifty.

Leading them out of his shed, he pushed the door shut, locking it out of habit. They jogged down the driveway, turned into the street and started picking up speed. By the time they reached the end of the street they had both fallen into the comfortable rhythm they had always shared when they ran. Eyes focused on the road, they automatically veered right to head for the showgrounds before pushing up the hill to the pole.

That's when they ran into another fence.

Zombies

This wasn't the same fence that had surrounded Nifty's compound; it was the rusty, sagging fence around Moran's Cove High School.

'How can this be?' said Deon. 'The high school's way over on the other side of town.'

'I can't imagine why you'd choose to add this to your scape,' said Nifty.

'I didn't.'

Across the footy oval, the school buildings looked deserted. The voices that had been in the distance earlier were now close. The shouts had become yowls, loud and urgent. They were coming from inside the school.

'Maybe we've crossed into someone else's scape,' said Deon. 'But whose?'

Without saying anything else, they turned away from the fence and ran southwest again, back towards the showgrounds, picking up the pace as they left the school fence behind them. They zigzagged through the deserted streets, turned at the memorial park and ran past a row of shops that looked like cardboard cut-outs. The corner of the showground road came into view up ahead. They turned left, running around the busted phone box on the corner, and were suddenly on sand. The air smelled salty, and small waves that shouldn't have been there lapped at the shore.

'The beach … we were nowhere near the beach.' Deon spun round instinctively to check on Nifty. His uncle was standing behind him, staring up at the sky and looking stunned.

Deon followed his gaze and saw ugly, dark storm clouds rocketing across the sky. They weren't coming from just one direction like clouds do when they're being blown by the wind. These clouds were scudding in from all directions at once. They were thick and dark and ominous, and they churned together until everything was blanketed in a thick gloom. The shadows stretched and blended into each other and flowed across the sand.

'I need a little help here,' Deon whispered to Node. 'I can't navigate through a scape I didn't even create.'

No answer. No flickering ghostly image.

'It's still Moran's Cove,' said Nifty. 'Let's just turn around and keep running.'

The yowling started again. Now it was all around them.

'It sounds like some kind of animal. And it sounds hungry.' Nifty scanned around through the gloom. The yowls were converging on the beach. The cries echoed out of the bushes and from behind the abandoned kiosks. 'Why would there be animals in here?' he said.

'Who dreamed this up and coded it?' said Deon. 'Do they really want the information that's in your head that badly?'

They backed towards the waterline, watching the beach shadows for signs of movement. The water felt real and wet as it lapped at their heels.

'Maybe we could swim out of here,' said Deon.

Then the yowls were behind them, and they spun around. Something was floating in the swell. As the grey water jostled up and down, wet heads bobbed up and down as the waves rose and fell.

Yowls from the beach again. They turned towards the shore, this time they saw the source of the sound. Shuffling slowly across the sand wearing shredded mouldy wetsuits were figures that looked to Deon to be surf zombies. Turning back towards the sea, he saw three more tattered surfers standing in knee-deep water. They trudged through the shallow waves, dragging their boards towards the beach. Nifty and Deon edged back onto the sand, looking back and forth from one group to the other.

As the beachside zombies lurched down to the water, Deon recognised their faces.

'Johno!'

'Who?' Nifty asked.

'It's Johno and his dumb mates.'

'What?'

'These guys are from school,' he said, gesturing at the ragged shuffling zombies, 'the real Moran's High. Remember I told you they'd been hassling me, getting a bit physical?' Deon couldn't help laughing at the irony.

'Explain,' said Nifty.

'Johno is sort of their leader, and they follow him around like brainless zombies, doing whatever he tells them to do. But they're back in our time. They can't be projecting into the plexus because they're not here.'

Nifty squeezed Deon's arm. 'That means you made them. You're the only one that could have coded all this detail.'

'But why are they coming after you?' asked Deon.

'I don't think it's me they're coming after, boy genius.'

'Me? But why?'

'You said they'd been hassling you. It wasn't just on the bus that day, was it?'

Deon flinched, remembering the maths classes, the locker room, his bike, hiding out at school, the game of brainiac ball on the bus. 'It's been happening for a while. I didn't tell Mum about it because she's got enough going on. And it wasn't that bad. I really thought it wouldn't last that long.'

'Well, it must've been bad enough for your subconscious to turn them into attack zombies.' Nifty put his arm around Deon's shoulders and squeezed. 'You should have told me sooner.'

Deon shrugged. 'I tried to ignore it, put up with it until I became too boring for them to bother with. Or until I could figure out a solution.'

Johno and his desiccated zombie mates shambled slowly towards them from both sides. With each lurching step, strings of drool swung back and forth from their ragged mouths.

'I've got to give you credit, boy genius,' said Nifty, 'you've conjured up some great zombies. Now can you conjure up a solution?'

Deon shrugged. 'They don't move that fast. We should try running again.'

'Running seems to get us nowhere, let's try something else,' said Nifty, his eyes sparkling with mischief.

'I have limited experience as a zombie hunter,' said Deon.

'I've watched a few zombie movies,' Nifty said.

'What's the best way to stop zombies?'

'Head trauma.' A huge smile spread across Nifty's face.

'Okay. I know this is only my mindscape and the zombies are only figments of my tortured imagination, but head trauma it is.' Deon crouched down in the wet sand and formed a ball, adding more sand until it was the size of a soccer ball. He smoothed the ball, and as he did, he felt it harden to glass in his hands. 'They don't have much brain to target, but let's see how *they* like being the target in brainiac ball.'

'Like they did to you on the bus?' Nifty started forming a ball of his own.

'Exactly.' Deon let fly with the glass sandball. It screamed through the air and dropped short of its zombie target, instead smashing through one of the zombie's surfboards.

A tortured howl ripped from the zombie's drooling mouth. 'Not … the … board!'

All the zombies froze and stared at the crushed surfboard. They slumped, dropped their heads into their hands and sobbed. Some buckled at the knees.

'Too funny,' said Nifty. 'Love the surf-zombie trope, boy genius.' He pelted his own ball at one of the sagging zombies. It was a direct hit, right to the forehead. There was a wet thud as the ball hit the side of its head. The shredded figure wobbled and devolved to pixel fragments, which exploded, leaving a glimmering fog of light and sparks of static that drifted down and dissolved into the sand.

'Nice!' Deon shaped another ball, squeezed it into glass and lobbed it. Another zombie exploded.

'Eight green zombies, shuffling on the beach,' Nifty sang as he formed a second ball.

Deon sang along with him as he shaped another ball. 'Eight green zombies shuffling on the beach.'

They both targeted and threw.

'If two of those zombies should purposefully fall …' sang Deon.

'… there'll be six green zombies, shuffling on the beach,' sang Nifty.

'It doesn't rhyme,' laughed Deon, as he threw again.

'It doesn't matter, it's poetry.'

There were only two zombies left. Deon and Nifty had worked their way up the beach. Deon's mind was buzzing as he made what he thought might be the last weaponised glass sandball. He'd tried the pacifist thing for too long at school; this felt really good.

Well aware that he couldn't inflict head trauma at his school, he resolved to find a way of getting some control, of finding some way to stop the surf zombies' bullying, when he got home again. The zombies' reaction to the broken surfboard was primal; they really loved their surfboards, a lot. Maybe learning more about surfboards might help Deon get some kind of strategic advantage over the zombies.

Nifty and Deon stood for a moment, indulging in a brief face-off with the last two zombies, Johno and a fat one that Deon thought might have been called Grunk. They let the last two balls fly. They sailed through the air, smacked into Johno and Grunk's heads … but the zombies did not fall down. The sandballs fell to pieces like … sand.

'This is your code, Deon. Why has it stopped working for you?'

'No clue,' said Deon.

Johno growled and stared. He stopped shambling and leapt towards Deon, slamming him down on the sand. He lay on him and pressed his forearm against Deon's throat. Deon's face was sprayed with sand as Nifty was slammed down onto the beach next to him. Nifty bucked and kicked under zombie Grunk's chunky wetsuit-clad body.

Deon kicked up hard at Johno, trying to hit something vital and painful, without any luck. Then he hunched his shoulders forward to get the pressure off his throat. Zombie Johno was winning. Deon's vision started sparking with splotches of random colour, and then everything started darkening around the edges. At the limits of his fading vision, he saw something flash through the sky.

'Better, faster, stronger.'

'Glide!' Deon choked out.

Her outstretched wings rippled with luminescent colour against the dark, roiling clouds. They ruffled and doubled in size as she plummeted out of the sky. Just as the image of the wings filled what was left of Deon's darkening vision, there was a buffeting of air against his face. Glide turned sharply and hovered, wings shimmering. A gleaming blade of light extended from the tip of her right wing. She flicked her elongated wing and the light-knife fizzed through Grunk's scull. An instant later, it sliced through Johno's. The pixel explosions left strobing shadows of light across Deon's vision, and Johno's weight was gone in an instant.

Deon sucked salty air into his hungry lungs.

'Huggy dance?' said Nifty, smiling at Deon and brushing sand off himself.

'Later,' coughed Deon.

Glide did a tight three-sixty-degree turn and landed.

'Nice wings,' Deon croaked.

'I thought I'd try something fancy in here. It'll be back to camouflage-chic when I get home.'

'Thanks for the help.' Deon stood up and reached to steady himself against Nifty. The beach had faded and they were standing at the busted phone box again.

'You're welcome.' She shrugged. 'It was an easy recovery. Let's go, zombie slayers, Node is waiting.'

'If Node wants us to hurry, how about another hoverbike?' asked Deon.

Nifty smiled and nodded.

'No more hoverbikes—or fancy wings.' Glide's wings faded back to green-brown. 'Let's just sneak out of here. Start running. I'll circle round and keep an eye out. See you at the pole.' She sprang up into the sky and flapped away.

Deon and Nifty ran after her, heading up the hill, out of the conjured Moran's Cove and out of the plexus. As they reached the pole, Glide circled it and winked out. Then Nifty faded. The wave of dizziness that came with moving in and out of the plexus washed over Deon. Then everything slowed, and felt thick and warm. He was alone.

Node

'Deon, mate, wakey-wakey.'

Deon's muscles ignored his attempts to move. His heart pounded. This didn't feel like just waking up. He hadn't been asleep, had he? He strained to remember. Before this he'd been in his mindscape with Nifty. They'd been running and Glide was above them. Then she disappeared and Nifty had melted away.

'Up you get, boy genius,' said Nifty.

Deon struggled to pull himself up to wakefulness. What had happened in the plexus? Glide and Nifty had reached the broken telegraph pole in the scape and vanished. Deon had reached the pole a second later, and everything had darkened and thickened around him. The familiar dizziness was there, but he felt like he'd taken a detour on the way out. Wherever he had stopped, the others hadn't been there.

He had been alone and there had been sounds, flashing images, words: a jostling, fast-slow swirling of information. There was a message, something important. He could still feel the importance of the message, but he could remember none of the words, and he knew there had been lots of them. Whatever the message was, it had been forced into his brain. His head felt too big on the inside.

'Up and at 'em, soldier—over.'

Deon opened his eyes. A circle of faces smiled down at him. His eyes locked on his uncle's face. 'Nifty, you're really all right.'

'Thanks to you.' Nifty leaned over and wrapped Deon in a hug.

Everyone else piled onto the bed and joined in. 'Huggy-hug-hug-huuug,' they chanted, squeezing together until Deon groaned. Then they took the hint and climbed off.

Nifty handed Deon some water and he gulped it down. 'More?' asked Nifty.

Deon coughed and nodded. 'I was stuck there, after you and Glide left the plexus.' He drank more slowly this time. 'I tried to follow and everything slowed down. I heard a voice …'

Nifty suddenly had his top-secret face on.

'What's up?' asked Deon.

'Nothing.' Nifty shook his head. 'I'm curious, what did this voice say?'

'It was fast. The message felt large and important. I can't remember, but … it was Node telling me …' Deon groaned. 'I can't remember … except … he wants to see me.'

'I'll call Link or Fuse for you,' said Nifty.

'No.' Deon shook his head. 'He wants to see *me*. And he wants me to see him.'

'Are you sure?' Nifty stammered. 'Maybe this is all happening because you were in the plexus.'

'You've been allowed to see him, Nifty. He asked to see me, I swear he did.'

'Node does want to see him,' Link added. 'You good to go now, Deon?'

'Absolutely.' Deon slid off the bed. He felt an echo of pain in his foot from when he'd clipped the shed with the hoverbike, but other than that he felt okay, strong even.

'Let's go, then,' said Link.

Nifty went to follow them.

'Just Deon for now,' said Link, gesturing for Nifty to stay. 'I'll come back for you soon, Nifty.'

Nifty nodded, his face drained of colour.

'What's up with Nifty? He looks like he's seen a ghost,' Deon asked Link as they walked towards the passage that led deeper into the cave.

'He's probably nervous for you. Seeing Node for the first time can be a bit hard to handle. Getting to know him and everything. His nature is fairly … weird.'

Deon walked next to Link along the dimly lit tunnel. He swallowed; his throat felt like sandpaper. He coughed, it sounded squeaky and strangled.

'Weird,' mumbled Deon. 'Well, no offence, but since I've met my new and very cool cyborg friends, who have genetically modified drop-bears for pets and live in high-tech treehouses, I'm getting used to weird. I think that meeting Node will give me a chance to complete my set of weird souvenirs from my time-travel holiday. I think I can handle it.'

'Cool,' was all Link said as they continued deeper into the cave.

The tunnel roof was much lower and smoother here. The space looked like it had been dug out of the rock purposefully. At the end of the passage, a thick metal door was slightly open. Deon realised only then that, apart from the two glass rooms and the tiny bathroom, there hadn't been any doors in the rest of the cave, just some folding partitions and lights that could be dimmed to provide a little privacy. In comparison, this door was massive, with an array of imposing locks studded across its surface. The frame that held it was anchored deeply into the surrounding rock of the cave walls.

Pushing through the half-open door, they entered a round chamber with a smooth wall and a low, domed ceiling. Against the wall on the opposite side of the room was a long curved bank of metal and lights. In the centre of the curve was a gleaming cylinder about a metre high and a metre wide. A web of glowing fibre-optic cables spilled over from some unseen connection point on top of the cylinder and sprawled outward, connecting at many points along the curved structure. The cables pulsed with a rhythm that felt to Deon more organic than mechanical.

'I brought Deon in like you asked,' Link said, speaking towards the glowing cluster of cables.

Deon scanned the length of the metal arc. There was no obvious interface point, no fake face on a screen. He couldn't see a place he should be aiming his conversation at.

'Thanks, Link,' said a quiet, very un-mechanical voice from the centre of the arc.

'Good to finally see you in the flesh, Deon.' The voice was slightly musical and full of human tone and inflection. Deon had helped make voices for his team bots at his old school in the city, so he knew that recorded words could be processed through a sound mixer to create convincing short phrases. But Node's voice sounded like the real deal, and it had even told a bad joke.

'H-hello,' stammered Deon. 'I'm so glad I finally get to … meet you.'

Node let out a quiet, musical chuckle. 'Me, too, although at first I was shocked to discover you were here. But now I'm stoked that I get to see you.'

'Stoked? You don't sound much like an AI. Is the phrasing and tone modelled on a real person's? I'm feeling a bit lost in the uncanny valley. I feel I should be more creeped out that you sound so real, but I'm not.'

'Well, I think he's handling things fine.' Link patted Deon on the shoulder.

'I think you're right,' said Node.

'I'm out of here.' Link turned and started walking away.

'Thanks again, Link,' said Node. 'I haven't seen any sign of Notz action, but if there's anything on the sensors I'll let you and Fuse know.'

Link nodded and left. For a split second Deon wanted to follow him.

'Sorry about the questions I've been asking.' Deon felt self-conscious all of a sudden.

'Don't apologise, Deon. Everything's always a question with you, and that's excellent.'

'How do you sound like that?' asked Deon.

'Right, the uncanny-valley thing.' said Node. 'As you can see, obviously I'm not even close to mimicking human action, but I've tried to make the tone of my voice as pleasant as possible because I rely on people listening to me. Following directions.'

'And your language program includes words like *stoked* and *excellent*. That seems like pretty elaborate programming.'

'All the better to express my unique personality.' Node chuckled again.

'Personality? How can you have a personality?'

'I was designed as a work in progress, Deon. I've been progressing ever since the warm, so I've had time to make some awesome improvements.'

'Awesome.' Deon shook his head. Again, every answer he got created three more questions. 'So …'

'But enough about me,' Node said. 'I asked you in here to thank you, and to try and repay you somehow for the outstanding help you offered.'

'Thanks for the offer, but I would've done anything to help Nifty.'

'You let me put a plug in the back of your head, mate, which goes above and beyond.'

'I did it for Nifty.'

'I know how important he is to you,' Node said quietly. 'You guys being here, in this time, and doing what you're doing, will make a difference.'

'*Will* make a difference?'

'Um … I mean *has* made a difference. Anyway, having you here has helped me—I mean us—and maybe the time you've spent here will help you, too. Things aren't so easy for you at the new school.'

'How do you know that?'

There was a momentary hum. 'Nifty told me. Maybe I can help with that. My way of saying thank you.'

'How can you help? That's all happening in your past.'

'We can make a plan, come up with a workable solution.'

'Like?'

'Surfboards,' said Node.

'How will surfboards help? I don't surf and I can't believe I ever will,' Deon said firmly.

'How about learning surfboard design? Make a board they can't resist that's better, faster, stronger.' Node laughed.

Deon blew out a long breath as he flashed back to his rushed, half-formed idea about surfboards in the plexus. 'Too weird.'

'What's weird?'

'Nothing.'

'So, what do you think? Learn board design and it could change your life.'

'If I say yes, what happens then? I know I'm smart, but wouldn't learning the subtle aqua-dynamics of board design take a while?'

'You could take a download.'

Deon rubbed the data port that was hidden under his hairline.

'By doing a download I can teach you everything I know about surfboard design in about forty-five seconds. Then you can go home and become the most sought-after shaper in the history of Moran's Cove. Zombie Surfboards will be open for business. You'll make a fortune—'

'You said "Zombie Surfboards". How do you know about the zombies? You said you don't go into the scape. How do you know?'

'Word travels fast in this place.' Node's voice sounded shaky.

Deon wondered how Node's voice could sound shaky. What would cause this large pulsing machine to sound nervous? His suspicions were growing. Node seemed to be zigzagging around, holding back, and being selective with the information it was willing to offer. Deon felt like he was trying to piece together an invisible jigsaw puzzle. Ideas and hunches were prickling at his intuition.

'I don't really understand your structure or your programming, but I can't help noticing you seem very fond of Nifty. So fond that you invented a time machine and then used it to scoop him from the past so you could see him.'

'That was all about the virus. I had to get him to help me to protect the Havz from the blue-ring.'

'But you're Node, you made the plexus. You *are* the plexus, so you know everything there is to know in this random place. How come you needed Nifty?'

'I needed Nifty because he was the one who could help me think the way I needed to think about the problem. He knew the problem from the ground up.'

'I'm not buying your reasoning.'

'He never wanted to develop that virus in the first place. I knew he would be glad to have the chance to help with the antivirus and see that the thing he never wanted to do had been undone.'

'So, you knew how he felt about it. How did you know that if you just met him?'

Node whirred quietly and sighed. 'It was just a p-presumption,' Node stammered. 'I based my hunch on the files I scanned.'

'How can an AI have hunches?'

'It's just a turn of phrase.'

'Which you use so you sound normal to listen to.'

'That's it, but let's get back to your thank-you gift. Do you want the info? Making surfboards could be quite a lucrative venture.'

'Okay, you can do the download.' Deon thought of the strategic advantage he could gain over the zombies, but he just said, 'I guess it would be good to get rich.'

Link walked back in through the half-open door. 'Node says you're opting for a download. Come on over here and get comfy.' He led Deon to a narrow bed and gestured for him to lie down. 'I'll just plug you in.'

'Plug me in?'

'No plugs, Deon,' said Node. 'It's just a ... turn of phrase.'

'It's a magnetic contact pad.' Link held up a small round disc that was attached to a wire.

Deon lay down, fidgeting. Link lifted his head and he felt a slight pressure on his neck, then a tingling. 'What does getting a download feel like?'

'It feels like taking a nap,' Link said, as the room faded to black.

Download

During Deon's unexpected nap, he dreamed of surfboards: algorithms, geometrics, deck curves, dovetails, fin sweeps and foils. Skittering around the edges of information were notions of business structure and marketing, website design, brands, logos, T-shirts. The data spun and floated, then drifted until it found a place to settle, shifting into new niches on the fringes of his memory. He blinked awake and stared up at the domed ceiling. The back of his neck felt warm.

'How long did I sleep?' he asked.

'Like I said, about forty-five seconds,' Node said.

Deon yawned like he'd been asleep for a week. He stood and stretched, then walked around in front of Node.

'How do you feel?' Node asked.

Deon smiled. 'Like a gnarly entrepreneur.'

'Gnarly dude.' Node chuckled. 'Are you good to go home and put your business plan into action?'

'Yeah.' Deon suddenly felt homesick for this place and these amazing people. 'I can come back though, right? You brought me here twice already, so—'

'I hadn't intended to bring you here at all,' Node said. 'That was just a mistaken DNA match. The scanner had a glitch and they scooped you instead of Nifty.'

'Well, that proves it's easy to do, so next time—'

'You won't be coming back, Deon. Not like that, anyway.' Node sighed.

'What other way can there be for me to come here? This is the future.'

'Do you know about the bootstrap paradox?'

'Yeah, Heinlein's story about the future affecting the past which can then affect the future, like a time loop,' said Deon.

'And the actions a person takes in the future will affect the past in a way that changes it … forever,' Node added.

'So maybe when I chose to get the aug, I changed things.' Deon touched the back of his neck and forced the squeak of desperation out of his voice. 'Then maybe I could come back somehow.'

'Coming to the future and choosing the aug has obviously changed your life from the way it was, but …' Another sigh.

'But what?'

'But you still have choices. You'll always have control over deciding your own future. You will be the one in charge of writing your own story.'

'What do you mean?' Deon's heart was thumping. He could feel the blood pulsing at his temples and at the

211

site of his new data port. 'If it's my future, I have a right to know.'

'Curiouser and curiouser.' Nifty's voice echoed from the dark edges of the cave behind Deon. He walked up and gently touched the port in the back of Deon's neck. 'How's it all going, boy genius?' he asked, but he was staring towards Node and suddenly his expression hardened.

'You have every right to know, Deon, and actually you already have all of the answers and info on board,' Node said.

Deon stared at Nifty, who was still staring hard at the big metal cylinder that housed Node. Deon followed his gaze to a position on the metal case, where two optical units sat side by side. He hadn't noticed them before among the general massive strangeness, but as he stared at them now they appeared to stare back, really stare. They glinted with an eerie awareness and familiarity.

There was an electrical fizzing inside Deon's head and a tingling at his aug site. 'What information do I have on board?'

'I uploaded three files. One with all the things you'll need to know to design gnarly surfboards so you can gain the upper hand with the surf bullies and make masses of cash to fund any future aspirations you may have.'

'What else will I be aspiring to?' asked Deon.

'I'm not a fortune teller.' Chuckle. 'Only you will know that, Deon.'

Nifty interrupted. 'What are these other files? I thought you were only downloading the board stuff.'

'One is a bit of an app I gave Deon.' Node laughed. 'It'll let you track Johno and his mates through the GPS on their phones. That way you can avoid them until you get the business going and they start treating you like the god of board design.'

'How do you know all the details for this? You'd need to know names and phone numbers, stuff I've never told you.'

'I've spent a lot of time in your head,' Node said.

Nifty coughed loudly and glared at Node.

Deon looked from Nifty to Node. 'What?'

'I was in your head,' Node stammered. 'When we were in the scape together the first time you went in. Then when you were in there searching for Nifty, I watched what went on as much as I could.'

Nifty closed his eyes and nodded.

'You said the download had three files,' said Deon. 'What's the third?'

'Well ... that one is a personal history,' said Node.

'So I can access all the data about you, cool.' Deon immediately tried recalling Node-related facts. He felt the electric fizz again.

'Slow down, Deon,' said Node, with a chuckle. 'I've encrypted that file, and I've attached a sly little device I invented. You won't be able to get that file open with a code or password. It will only ever be opened at the time when you do the thing, and think the thing that signals to the file that you're ready to receive that information.'

Nifty shook his head, half smiling. 'So he may never get the file open,' he said, looking relieved.

'Right, Nifty, maybe he never will. Everyone has the right to decide their own future. Deon will make his own decisions, but if he needs that information the file will open.'

'So, I came to the future and now I have possession of a file full of information that could affect the past … which will be my future.' Deon tapped the side of his head. 'And I'll take that file with me to the past and the file will be there in my head, but it might never open and never play a part in my future.'

'That's the time loop, my friend,' said Node. 'If the future is supposed to affect the past, it will.'

'But this *is* the future, so you should already know my future, which is now the past. Do you know what happens?'

'Stop asking questions, Deon, you haven't had your future yet,' said Node.

Nifty slung his arm heavily around Deon's shoulders and interrupted the twisting chain of enquiry. 'So when are we heading back?'

'After the party,' Node said.

'Party?'

'Celebration, farewell party. You've been a great member of the team, Deon. We're all going to miss you.'

'Then let me come back sometimes, just for a visit,' Deon tried again.

'Can't do it, Deon. Using the time scoop makes us more noticeable to the Notz than we can afford to be. It attracts them to the base.'

'But you took the risk … twice. I'm glad you did.'

'Me, too.' Sigh. 'I can't tell you how great it's been to have both of you here, but you've got a life to live, Deon, and some surf zombies to control back in real time.' Node fell silent for a long moment and Nifty stared into the glistening, mechanical eyes.

'How long do we have?' asked Nifty quietly.

'We'll party tonight and fling you back in the morning,' said Node.

Deon sighed. He couldn't bear saying anything that sounded like goodbye. This, here and now, felt like real time to him. Moran's Cove had never felt more unreal.

'Having you here has been amazing, Deon.' Node sighed. 'And Nifty, I couldn't have done it without you. I couldn't have done any of this without you.'

Nifty just stood staring into Node's eyes.

Deon walked away towards the door; neither Nifty nor Node noticed him leave.

Talent Show

The wall of water that hid the path outside the cave burbled endlessly. Deon stood watching the film of blue-green water slide by, letting the sound and movement fill his mind. The ferns and vines on either side of the path leading down from the cave were already springing back into place after Bump's shoving. By this time tomorrow, there would be no sign of the track. Deon drew a shuddering breath. By this time tomorrow, all this would be centuries away.

The sun was low by the time he reached South Bower and the valley was filling with dark-green shadow. Above him, he could see small points of light escaping between the leaves of the thick canopy as the breeze shifted the branches. The water churned and tumbled away down the falls. Deon breathed in the cool moist air as he sat in the sling of the rappel chair and shrugged himself into the harness.

The rhythmic effort of hauling himself back up the tree trunk let him work all the tension of this almost unbelievable day out of his muscles. South Bower was in darkness. He decided everyone must be at North Bower for the party. He took a zip-line trolley off the shelf, leaned against the railing and looked towards the top of the falls, in the direction of the hidden cave.

What was keeping Nifty?

'One man, so many secrets,' Deon mumbled, as he clicked the trolley in place and climbed over the railing. He pushed off and flew across the narrow valley, trying to take his time.

When he arrived, Glide was waiting at the railing with Bump.

'Now it's party time—over.'

'Thank you so much for … for my recovery, Deon.' Glide leaned out over the railing and hugged him.

'You're welcome.' Deon looked back out at the cable silhouetted against the last colour of the day.

'Can't help noticing you haven't unhooked your trolley from the line,' said Glide.

'No, I haven't.' He stood staring back across to South Bower. 'Riding the zip-line never gets old.'

'Go again—over.'

'Yes, why not?' said Glide. She sniffed at Deon and smiled. 'But let me remind you of our no-stink policy.'

'Understood.' Deon smiled broadly and took off, zinging back across the zip-line in the near darkness. Then he returned, jumped straight over the railing and headed for the showers before he was tempted to have one more turn.

Halfway back down the spiral stairs, Deon met Nifty heading up. 'It took you a while to finish up. Problems?'

'Um, we were just wrapping up the last of the blue-ring stuff before we go home,' said Nifty. 'Glide is on stink patrol, so I'll be back soon.' Nifty raced up the stairs.

Deon couldn't remember every hearing Nifty say 'um' before. What was his uncle holding back? He leaned on the curved banister and ran his fingers across the spikey stubble at the back of his neck, where they had shaved some of his hair away before sliding the aug under his skin. There was a slightly tender incision, glued closed, and beneath it was the raised circle of his data link.

He knew that all the answers Nifty wasn't offering would probably be in the downloads; at least Deon guessed they would be. He hoped he'd know it all one day. He just needed to think the right thoughts to unlock the file.

'Like looking for a mental needle in a haystack,' he mumbled. He also knew it might take him the rest of his life to think of the one specific thought that would open the file.

The hair would grow back and hide the data link, but Deon would have to hide the aug for the rest of his life. Node had told him it wouldn't show up in medical tests or scans with present-day medical technology, so unless he had actual surgery no one would see it. Travelling to the future had absolutely affected the past ... and that was where he had to create his future.

'Deon, the party's down here, mate, you can't dance on the stairs,' Throttle called. 'Node sent me over a file of new, well, old tunes.' He waved the small control pad they had used for vid files on robot night. 'So it's DJ Throttle in the house.' He ran the control pad up and down the thigh rod on his augz frame, and a sound like a turntable scratch came out of the speakers on the wall.

Bump and Retro pushed back the furniture, Fuse dimmed the lights, and Throttle scratched and mixed his way through the centuries-old playlist as they all danced together in the treetops. Everyone was laughing, and Deon found himself wondering what things had been like for these guys back in the Notz city, before they had the chance to get auged. What would their lives have been like if it hadn't been for Node?

Fizz. He felt a small brain fizz and inhaled sharply. Was that thought part of the right idea?

Nifty joined the dance party. He started chanting in time with the beat. 'Hug.' He stomped. 'Hug.' Held his arms out wide. 'Hug-hug-hug.' He danced around, catching them all up in his hugging, chanting circle until everyone was linked arm in arm in a clumsy dance.

'Hug!' they yelled, stamping the beat. 'Hug!' Scratching the rhythm. 'Hug-hug-hug!' Until they tripped over each other, and fell onto the floor in a laughing pile of hugs.

The light brightened. 'I've captured it all,' said Fuse, tapping at his temple. 'These will be great to add to your souvenir files, Deon.'

'You … I can do that?'

'Yeah, easy, I'll collect some more during the talent show after dinner and send them to you later.'

'Just like that.'

'Yep. You're one of us now.'

I am a brainiac, Deon thought. Maybe he could find a way to connect to things when he got home. If he could learn more, maybe he could invent a way to link to … a phone. *Fizz*. Deon knew he was onto the right idea.

'Food's ready—over.'

'You okay?' Nifty took Deon's arm and steered him over to the table.

'Yeah, I'm really okay.'

'Hungry?'

'Starving.' Deon smiled, and let thoughts of food fill his mind.

It was a feast of pizza and dump-chook nuggets, garlic bread and a salad with a wicked chilli dressing. Everyone ate until they were stuffed.

'I scream, you scream—over.' Bump served bowls piled high with the delicious ice cream that wasn't.

'We might scream, all right, Bump,' Nifty said, rubbing his bulging stomach.

They all managed to squeeze in the ice cream. Then they waddled around doing the dishes and tidying up. Scout started shoving the furniture back into place from their pre-dinner dancing.

'The next order of business,' said Scout, 'is the talent show. We want Deon to have an awesome file to take home with him. We want that file to show the many talents of the amazing, astounding, stupendous Havz.'

'Memories of a lifetime—over.'

'Exactly. We want this to be a talent show worthy of being remembered forever, coz he can't delete it.' Scout bowed. 'A little humour to liven up the crowd,' he said. 'Havz and Havenots—sorry, Nifty—go and make your preparations for the talent show. We meet at the sofas in ten.'

It was definitely a show to remember. It started with Glide whistling the quollagoes to come inside and display their gene-mod, marsupial cleverness with an impressive display of tricks she had taught them. Next, Retro did a juggling act using a collection of spare augz components. Link and Fuse did their entertaining and educational impersonations of extinct species they had researched in the archives.

Bump did an unexpected tap-dance routine, and to Deon's surprise, he wasn't at all clumsy. 'Singing in the rain—over.'

Throttle tied a T-shirt across his eyes and had Nifty check he really couldn't see. Then he folded a paper crane blindfolded.

'Very impressive,' said Nifty.

'I had lots of time to practise after my accident.' Throttle took a bow and sat down. 'You're up, Deon.'

Deon had decided to show off his talent as a trivia mastermind, specialty subject *Dr Who*. 'I'll recite all the doctors in order. Hartnell, Throughton, Pertwee, Baker, Davison, the other Baker, McCoy, McGann, Eccleston,

Tennant, Smith, Capaldi, Whittaker and where to place John Hurt.' He shrugged and bowed, and started straight into reciting the doctor's companions in order. Next he described the many and varied adversaries the doctor had faced, referencing their planets of origin and the most effective way to vanquish them, or at least make them run home to their own planet or dimension.

'We need to remember the cybermen for the next robot night,' said Scout.

'Not really robots—over.'

'Node says well done,' said Link. 'He also said you'll love the next couple of doctors.'

'Tell me more,' said Deon.

'Node says "spoilers".' Link shrugged.

Nifty laughed.

'It's your turn, Nifty,' said Glide. 'What have you got planned?'

'Node and I are going to do a duet,' said Nifty.

'Say again?' said Deon.

'I said Node's going to accompany me while I sing one of my playlist favourites.'

The lights dimmed and the room filled with soft guitar music. Deon had recognised the song by the fourth chord change. It was one of Nifty favourites. It was the one he had been hum-mumbling on and off since they'd arrived here.

Nifty stared into some personal, faraway place as he sang, starting quietly. Everyone listened, captivated by the gentle power of the song.

Link was quietly singing along.

'How do you know this song?' whispered Deon. 'It's from centuries ago.'

'I've heard Node playing and singing it up in the cave. I'm in there a lot so I've heard it a lot. I guess I just learned it.'

Node's voice slid in alongside Nifty's and he smiled, still looking to somewhere no one else could see. The two voices wove together, rising and falling, back and forth, like they'd sung this song together many times. Node's voice swelled and Nifty's faltered, then their voices melded together. When the song faded away, Nifty wiped the tears from his face as the lights brightened.

Deon was puzzled. Node already knew this song. He really knew it. *Fizz.*

'We've got a surprise for you guys,' said Glide. 'Let's have some hot chocolate and we'll tell you all about it.'

Everyone crowded around the table as Glide and Scout passed around mugs of the Milo-like hot drink.

'After you've gone back,' Glide said, 'and the scoop's still powered up we're going to send you a present.'

'Why not just give it to us to take now?' asked Deon.

'Where's the fun in that?' said Throttle.

'We've put together a reverse time capsule,' added Retro.

'Reverse?' said Deon.

'Yeah, reverse. People usually place things in a time capsule and seal it, and then it's opened in the future, but instead we're going to send something back in time.'

'How will we find it?'

'We'll give you the clues—over.'

223

'We know where and when we're going to hide it,' said Glide. 'It'll be up to you two to figure out the clues and search for it. If you find it, you get your surprise. Listen up, here come your clues.'

Everyone except Deon and Nifty started to chant the riddled clues.

'Up high and down low,

Where it's cold, but there is no snow.

It can't burn, but it boils,

It gives reward for your toils.

Where one thing ends, but the other begins,

Not everything that glitters has tails and fins.'

'—over.'

'That's it?' asked Deon.

'That's all you get—over.'

Glide was smiling broadly. 'Marshmallows, anyone?'

Replay

Deon sat alone at the table on the platform, staring out into the pitch-black night. The lights came on and he jumped. It was Fuse.

'Let's do that download,' Fuse said.

'Just like that?'

'Just like that. Get comfy.'

Deon sat on the sofa. He felt heat at the back of his neck and his mind swirled with images and words. They raced and jerked, jostling like mental bumper cars. His head felt too big. Nausea lifted the contents of his stomach. He swallowed hard. There was a screeching buzz and then everything inside his head went quiet.

'It might feel a bit disorienting,' said Fuse. 'Are you okay?'

'I think so.'

'Test the file.'

'How?'

'Just try and remember, but concentrate broadly, like you're looking for a book title on a shelf.'

The memories were mixed up, but they were there. Deon knew it was the file because all the images were from Fuse's point of view. He flicked through the visual feast until Fuse patted him on the shoulder.

'You should go to bed,' said Fuse, heading for the stairs. 'You can access them any time you want … forever.' Fuse walked up the stairs and the lights faded.

Deon stood and let his eyes adjust to the dark. Moonlight was poking through the canopy. The little spots speckled the darkness. He walked slowly up the stairs, trying to put every detail of this amazing place into his own memories. It had all really happened.

He moved through the hush of quiet breathing in the top level of the bower. I'm going home tomorrow, he thought. But this felt like home now, too. He rolled into his hammock and replayed his precious new memory file until he finally fell asleep.

'Hey, Deon.' Scout's voice sounded urgent. 'Node says now, and good morning.'

'Good morning,' said Deon, trying to focus. 'Is there a problem?'

Next to Deon, Nifty stretched and swung out of his hammock.

'No problems—over.'

'Nothing's wrong, Node just said it's better if you rip the Band-Aid off fast,' said Scout. 'Leave before you have time to hesitate.'

'Quick march—over.'

'So, grab your gear, we're off. See you down below,' said Scout. He and Bump turned and left.

'Let's pee and get going, boy genius,' said Nifty casually.

'You knew we'd leave in a hurry, didn't you?'

'It's easier for all of us.'

When they reached the bottom of the stairs Deon could see that the bower was empty. 'Not even a goodbye?' he said, as he strapped on his harness for his final rappel down the tree.

Nifty shrugged and climbed into his own harness.

Scout and Throttle were waiting at the base of the tree when Deon landed.

'Nifty's with me,' said Scout. 'You'll ride with Throttle.'

'Where is everyone?' asked Deon. 'I thought I'd at least get to say goodbye.'

'Goodbye—over.' Bump was somewhere within the thick wall of green.

'Bump! You spoiled the surprise,' said Retro.

All around, the leaves shook and the bushes laughed. Then the rest of the Havz, Deon's mates, burst out into the clearing.

'We wanted to surprise you with a proper farewell,' said Fuse.

'We're going with you to the scoop site,' said Glide.

'Cool!' said Deon.

'Move out—over.'

Glide sprang up and lifted into the sky. She whistled to Rex, Nelly and Cuddlepie, and they chittered and jumped along after her across the treetops. Link and Fuse lifted backpacks onto their shoulders and scrambled up onto Retro and Bump's backs. Deon and Nifty climbed up onto Scout and Throttle's back and secured their safety straps.

'Parade of honour—over,' said Bump, and they were off.

The huge leaps down the falls left Deon rattled and glad no one had offered him any breakfast to throw up. Once they were at the base of the falls, they all fell into a synchronised bounding procession through the dense trees towards the east.

The synchronisation didn't last long. Bump was the first to succumb to the temptation and leap over Retro and Link. They all cringed, waiting for Bump to land.

'Poor Fuse,' Throttle mumbled.

Bump landed, teetered and corrected. 'I'm fine—over.'

Everyone cheered. 'Well, there's a first time for everything,' said Throttle.

Retro picked up speed and bounced, and she and Link leapt high over Bump and Fuse. Full of confidence, Bump leaped again.

'Just so you know, Scout, I'm too old for leapfrog,' Nifty said.

But the crazy leapfrog frenzy continued, zigzagging through the tangle of green. When they stopped, Deon realised they had arrived. Just like that. This was it. Bump and Retro were already helping Link and Fuse unload their packs.

'Hate to be rude, guys,' said Link, 'but Node says he would rather neither of you look too closely at the scoop gear. Could you turn around, please?'

Deon laughed. 'Is Node worried we'll look at the scoop and figure out how to make it?'

'Top secret—over.'

'It'd probably take me two hundred years to figure out that stuff.' *Fizz*.

Glide rushed over and wrapped her arms around Deon and Nifty's shoulders. 'Can we have one last huggy dance?'

They all jammed in together, hugging and bouncing. Link and Fuse joined the tangle for one last squeezy hug. As they hugged, Deon noticed the air starting to fill with the familiar robot-like smell. Static was bristling, sparking. The world was tilting around them and becoming unsteady.

'Have you already switched it on?' Deon asked. 'Won't you guys get pulled in, too?' How great would it be if they could come back with me?

'There's no risk of us going with you,' said Scout. 'Remember, it's like an energy slingshot. We powered up the scoop and now it'll release you to be flung back to when you left.'

The world tilted even more. Deon's stomach churned and squeezed. Nifty wrapped his arms around Deon's shoulders as the pull-twist-pull motion became stronger. In that blurring, swirling moment it was all gone—the jungle, the smiling faces, the bright sunlight, everything. No, I'm wrong, Deon thought, correcting himself. It's Nifty and me who have gone away.

Scooped. Crackling static pressed and bounced around them, and prickling zaps earthed on them. The pull grew stronger before it flicked and released them.

In seconds it had all changed. They were lying in darkness, on the damp overgrown grass outside Nifty's shed.

The workbench light was on inside, just as it had been when Deon had dived for the shimmering mirage before he had been scooped to the future.

The mirage! Deon snapped his head around just in time to see the wobbly images of his friends waving at him as the shimmering portal shrank and blinked out.

Time Capsule

Deon and Nifty sent a message to Deon's mum saying they had gone fishing, and they decided to lay low and pretend they were actually away. They hung around Nifty's shed all weekend, telling and retelling their stories, comparing points of view, and trying to get a grip on the unreality of it all. It was hard to get the here and now of Moran's Cove to stop feeling weird after what they had experienced.

They distracted themselves by properly exploring Deon's downloaded knowledge. Deon asked Nifty to sacrifice some of his precious shed space and, using some old pieces of poly-foam packing Nifty had stored up in the shed rafters, he played around with some board shaping. His trial boards actually looked like boards. His life had already started to be affected by what he had brought back from the future.

But the fake fishing trip had to come to an end, and whether they felt ready or not, they had to accept that they were back home and life had to continue. Over that weekend, the bootstrap paradox had shown that it was already working to change things, and by the time Deon went to school on Monday, things had already started to get better.

The second file had opened and the app worked just like Node had bragged it would. At school, and anywhere around town, as soon as Deon's implant sensed one of the zombies' phones coming in on an intercept course, he received a sensation a little like a cold shiver down his spine. Then he changed direction or kept his head down until they passed.

Within a few weeks, he had become invisible again, which meant he could put all his efforts into developing his board-shaping skills. Once he had applied the downloaded design knowledge and shaped out the first of his boards, Nifty loaned him some start-up capital and he was ready to introduce the surfers of Moran's Cove to his designs.

Zombie Surfboards did a stealth launch online. Surfers got sent trial boards in exchange for them posting feedback on social media about the boards' performance. Word went out about Zombie Surfboards: exceptional design, very affordable. Deon's website started buzzing with enquiries, and orders were sent out up and down the coast.

Then, one blisteringly hot Saturday morning, Zombie Surfboards had its first pop-up event right there on the main surf beach at Moran's Cove. There were demos and board trials, free T-shirts and lots of hype as everyone speculated about the—up until now—anonymous person behind the new surfboard brand. As the event was wrapping up, they introduced the mystery board designer and CEO of Zombie Surfboards, and Deon's status around town was changed forever.

Deon's mum didn't care too much for his entrepreneurial success. She still expected him to study and win competitions, even though winning scholarships was no longer an issue now that Zombie Surfboards money would pay for university. And of course Deon had solid plans to go to university. He wanted to learn everything he could, and take advantage of every opportunity that came his way. He wanted to fill his head with every idea and thought he possibly could, because he didn't know what life experience or thought or new idea might be the one to unlock the encryption on the third file, and he *really* wanted to know what was inside that third file.

Zombie Surfboards became such a success that Deon had to expand. Nifty built a second shed and Deon employed some board shapers. Deon's mum could see that he was still making study a priority, so she offered her support and put her artistic skills to work designing logos, murals and t-shirts.

Deon's year had started off with the sadness of his dad dying. Then the year had morphed into the weirdness of that unreal time with Node and the Havz, and things kept changing. Finally, he started to feel that he belonged in Moran's Cove. He knew he had a future here. And somewhere in that future was the third file, lying locked inside his brain, waiting for the day when he might be able to open it.

Life smoothed out in Moran's Cove. Deon and Nifty even had a couple of tries at surfing, but they were so hopeless at it they thought it would be bad for business if people saw the brains behind Zombie Surfboards constantly wiping out, so they leaned the boards against the shed and went back to running.

Deon and Nifty picked up speed as they jogged down Nifty's street, and fell into that synchronised heartbeat rhythm that they shared. They turned at the showgrounds and headed up towards the broken pole that was still their turnaround point, the place that had turned both their lives upside down.

At the pole, they stopped to catch their breath. Staring up at the distant ridges, towards the craggy rock steps of the falls, Deon turned to Nifty and said, 'Hey, Nifty, do you want to go hiking? Head up to the steps and see if we can catch a fish?'

'It's been a while ...sounds great. When?'

'Next weekend?'

'It's a plan.'

They turned and ran back to town. Nifty mumbled something about camping gear and equipment. Deon tuned out and replayed the file of the talent show, and silently wished that somehow, when they walked up into the bush next weekend, he would hear Rex chitter, Glide would make her piercing whistle, and they'd all be there, in the trees at the steps waiting for him.

But he knew they couldn't be there. They wouldn't be there for more than two more centuries.

There was a tiny fizz in the back of his head as the video file finished. He thought of how much good work Scout and Link and the others were able to do because of the augz. Would that all happen? Would the augz really be developed? What would it take to connect the organic to the mechanical? Deon had been too busy with his boards to go down this mental trail before.

He felt the fizz again, tickling the inside of his skull. Thinking about the Havz and their tech had triggered regular brain fizzes. Deon was sure each fizz brought him a step closer to unlocking the third file. If he could find the time capsule, the surprise inside might be something that would help to unlock it. He ran on, smiling and mumbling the riddle to himself.

'Up high and down low,

Where it's cold, but there is no snow.

It can't burn, but it boils,

It gives reward for your toils.

Where one thing ends, but the other begins,

Not everything that glitters has tails and fins—over.'

The Third File

S aturday rolled around and they threw their gear into the back of Nifty's dilapidated ute and shambled out of town. Turning at the showgrounds, they drove past the broken pole and followed the twisting road up into the hills until it ended in a stump of tar that was swallowed by the rainforest.

They hauled their gear onto their backs and entered the almost overgrown track. Within seconds the rainforest had swallowed them and it was a sea of tangled green on all sides. Bright sunlight stabbed down through the treetops, striping the green with thin shards like frozen lightning bolts. Deon shrugged his pack into a comfortable position on his shoulders and fell into step behind Nifty.

The narrow path was spongy with fallen leaves. It was cool under the forest canopy. The air smelled of the sweet, complicated aliveness all around them. Deon took a deep breath.

Nifty began to hum. The hum grew into the familiar mumbled nineties playlist. Everything was just as it should be, normal. As normal as it would ever get, considering Deon had a data link in the back of his neck and an encrypted file hiding inside his head.

He was homesick for a place that wouldn't exist for another two centuries. *Fizz.*

He missed his mates, who had not been born yet. *Fizz.*

They might never become augmented. *Fizz.*

Deon's breath shuddered. He tripped over a gnarled tree root that had twisted up out of the soft ground. Nifty didn't hear Deon land in the leaf litter, and continued to mumble-hum his way up the track, leaving him alone. Deon leaned against the tree to catch his breath.

Fizzzzzzz. Node's file fizzed open. Time stretched, twisted, tangled inside Deon's head. He sat leaning against the tree with his heart clanging in his chest. Maybe it was all a joke, he thought.

There was only one path, so Deon knew he would catch up to Nifty somewhere up ahead and tell him what was in the file. Deon ran hard. His pack flopped up and down on his back, throwing him off balance. He rushed on, stripes of light strobing between the gaps in the trees. He stopped, gasping. The rainforest spun around him. This was unbelievable. How could he find the words to tell his uncle what he'd discovered in the file? He had to run. Run and think.

Shrugging off the backpack, Deon turned and sprinted back down the track. Jumping the gnarled root, he didn't slow down until the truck and the road came into view. He stopped. His whole body was drumming in time with his thumping heart. He felt fear, adrenaline, amazement, fear, pride, excitement, wonder. Now he was ready to share it all with Nifty. He turned and ran back up the path.

When Deon reached the clearing next to the lowest pool in the steps, Nifty was scraping rocks and sticks away to make a site to roll out the swags. Deon stood in the shadows watching, trying to quiet his shuddering breath.

This was their spot. Nifty and Deon's dad had come here as boys. Nifty and Deon had caught fish here with Glide's nets. Well, they would in the future. Now Deon and Nifty were here together.

Past. Future. Present.

The time-loop stuff that had already happened helped Deon believe that the amazing things Node had divulged in the encrypted file were true, or could be true if that's what Deon chose to do with his future. It was always going to be up to him to write his own story. He had a hunch that Nifty already knew some of that truth.

'Up high, but down low, where it's cold there is no snow,' Deon said, as he stepped into the clearing and sat down in a patch of sunshine next to Nifty.

'You took your time,' Nifty said.

'I've been thinking about things.' Deon shrugged off his pack and stared at the churning water in the pool. 'Water that can't burn, but it boils, giving reward for your toils,' he mumbled. 'Hey, Nifty, remember the last time we were here?'

'You mean, when we *will* be here,' corrected Nifty.

'Yeah, yeah, time, time. That day we thought we were going home and then you got captured and the whole rescue mission began—'

'Where one thing ended, but another begins,' said Nifty.

Deon stood and walked to the edge of the pool. 'Not everything that glitters has tails and fins—'

'Over,' said Nifty, following him.

The glint of sunlight on metal caught Deon's eye. He dropped down onto his knees and leaned out into the icy water, plucking the metal cylinder from a rock shelf just below the surface. The time capsule looked pristine, brand new, like it had just been placed there.

'They knew we'd be coming here, today or very soon.' Deon held up the shiny cylinder. 'It hasn't even been here long enough to tarnish.' He looked for footprints around the pool, or snapped branches where Bump might have crash-landed. If they had been there, the forest had already claimed any sign of them.

The metal slid smoothly as he unscrewed the end cap, then tipped the cylinder up and let the contents fall onto the grass. There was a handful of anagram tiles, a diagram for an ibis trap, and a note at the bottom: *They're so tasty it's worth the effort.*

There was a roll of brown-green fabric that Deon recognised as the embarrassing bike pants he had worn. And there was one of the flowers that Rex and Nelly and Cuddlepie had often stuck on their fur after their patrols through the canopy. The flower was fresh; the time capsule hadn't been here long.

Suddenly Deon felt heavy. His arms and legs felt as though they'd turned to rock. His heart squeezed. He was dizzy. 'I miss you guys,' he mumbled, and flopped down on the ground. The talent-show file booted without him accessing it, but he didn't mind at all. The fizz returned for a second.

'Are you okay?' Nifty sat next to him and slung an arm across his shoulders.

'They were right here, Nifty, maybe today or yesterday. They could've stayed for a while so we could say hi.'

'It doesn't work that way, Deon. They can fling things, but people can't be here, I mean now, unless they're from here.' He squeezed Deon shoulders. 'Huggy-hug,' he whispered under his breath.

'I could see them again,' Deon said quietly. 'That third file might tell me how.'

'Who knows, boy genius.'

'Aren't you curious enough to get that file unlocked?'

'I'm not sure. I guess it depends on what's in it.'

'Like you don't already know some of it.' Deon stared at Nifty.

Nifty's eyes grew wide and glassy. 'It's unlocked, isn't it?' Deon nodded.

'What's in it?' Nifty drew a rasping breath.

'Lessons about a history that hasn't happened yet,' Deon said, 'and a job offer. The weirdest career in the universe, I'm guessing.'

'What does Node want you to do?'

'He wants me to use what I know about all the damage industry is capable of doing to the environment in the future.' Deon tapped the port at the back of his neck. 'Node showed me the damage, and it's massive. He wants me to study, get rich and make a difference, stop the damage before it's too late.'

'That's a huge task.' Nifty ran his hand through his hair and sighed.

'Yep, but if it isn't doable Node has a plan B.'

'Which is?'

'Which is an anagram of Deon.'

'Run that by me again.' Nifty stared intently across the pond.

'Come on, Nifty, I watched how you reacted when you were with Node, you already know.' Deon stood up. 'Mild-mannered teenager, Deon becomes superhero, super-computer Node.'

Nifty went very pale and nodded his head slowly.

'That's why he scooped you and accidentally scooped me. That's why the Notz took you. They thought you were a way to get to Node, which you surely would have been. Either because of what you knew or as a hostage to make Node cooperate, because of how it feels about you.' Deon's breath shuddered.

'You don't ever have to do any of this, Deon.' Nifty hugged Deon tightly, then smiled and tapped Deon's head. 'So what do you really know? What's in there?'

'I have the bite-sized history of Node's future ... *my* future. The way it is this time, if we don't fix things before the damage is done.'

Nifty grimaced.

'And I know of sub-files, small hacks to get the environmental action started when the time's right.'

'So it'll be different and you won't have to … become Node.'

'Maybe not, the sub-files will open as I need them.'

'We have to make a difference,' said Nifty.

'If we can't, then one of the sub-files will tell me where the drive is hidden that will help me initiate the Node project, if none of the other strategies has worked.'

'You can't do that, Deon.' Nifty grabbed Deon's shoulders. 'You can't become Node.'

'I might never have to, but I can think of six or seven really good reasons why I would want to.'

'Surely the augz can be developed and the Havz can happen without you needing to become Node.'

'We can't know that yet, but I know enough for now, and we know where my cave is.'

'*Your* cave?'

'*Our* cave.'

They abandoned the camp at the low pool and hiked up the steps. Deon stopped at the third level, pacing around the underbrush.

'What are you looking for?' asked Nifty.

'Saplings,' said Deon. 'Crows ash, the type of trees the bowers were built in. We need to make sure they grow strong and healthy in this area, just in case.'

Nifty shrugged and smiled. 'Let's take a look at that cave.'

Deon followed him up the twisting, overgrown track that disappeared within the mass of green. Nifty hummed, Deon mumbled.

Epilogue

I n the years that followed, Deon realised some things. Surfers, just like Johno and his zombies, were very good at something else apart from surfing. They were passionate environmental activists and spread the word, helping to make real change. Zombie Surfboards grew and diversified as Deon learned where to invest the money he made to support others who were trying to do good work for the environment. Moran's Cove became a hub for environmental innovations and other developments Deon and Nifty never told anyone about.

Nifty remained good at keeping his tech secrets, the biggest one being Deon's data link. With the Zombie Surfboards money, Deon started researching and developing augmentations, knowing they would help many people one day, after they had been trialled and perfected. He volunteered to do most of the trails on himself. He liked the tweaks, and the extra connectivity. It meant he could reach out and tap into the best places to drop the hacks Node had stored in the third file—when the time was right.

Deon became a secret influencer where he could, reaching out with his new connections, watching to see how things were changing. What would turn out differently this time? He was keeping track of the new history that he was helping to create.

The environmental damage was slower than the records in Node's bite-sized history stated, so this future was different already. Deon would have to wait and see whether it would be different enough that he wouldn't need to become Node.

When things were quiet, he opened the files and remembered dancing while Throttle scratched on his frame and mixed tunes. Or he watched Retro juggling spare parts, or remembered the unexpected tastiness of dump-chook burgers. It had been an unreal time. There were times when Deon thought it might be an excellent thing to make the changes and complete his time loop to be with his awesome, auged mates again.

Acknowledgements

Thanks so much to the amazing Hayley Jackson for her *unreal* wisdom about all things timey-wimey. She offered the gift of candid feedback, which strengthened my story, and helped me make sure my time loops weren't tangled and that no one arrived anywhere in the story before they were born.

A huge shout-out to Micah Klokman for offering his unique insight to enrich my story and ensure it had adequate awesomeness. Micah is wise beyond his years. He has a strong sense of story and a massive imagination that he uses to create twisty tales. I hope to be able to return the favour and support him when he writes his first book one day soon.

As always, thank you to Anthony Puttee, Penny Springthorpe and the rest of the team at Book Cover Cafe for their creative insights and professional support.

About the Author

Martii Maclean lives in a tin shack by the sea, catching seagulls that she uses to make delicious pies, and writing weird stories. She likes going for long bicycle rides with her cat, who always wears aviator goggles to stop her whiskers blowing up into her eyes as they speed down to the beach to search for mermaid eggs.

To find out more about Martii, get your free short story, and discover her free resources for kids, teachers and writers, visit martiimaclean.com.

Other titles by Martii Maclean

If I Die Before I Wake
Not all tales have the ever-after you might expect. Vreni is sleeping-beauty's granddaughter and the sleeping curse has controlled every female in the family for centuries.

Weird Weirder Weirdest: A collection of quirky tales.
Come this way … meet a whispering cat, write with a magic pen, use a watch to stop time, take a step in magic shoes and meet the patchwork girl … it's not too far, just beyond the here and now.

We of the Between
When Trin sees blue people rise from the ocean she is destined to be drawn into the magical and dangerous place between two worlds.

The Adventures of Isabelle Necessary
A girl, a beachy town, lots of friends and oodles of adventures … come and have fun with Isabelle at Saggy Beach.

www.ingramcontent.com/pod-product-compliance
Lightning Source LLC
Chambersburg PA
CBHW021007120726
47905CB00009B/2894